HIS LORD'S SOLDIER

GREAT WAR SERIES
BOOK FOUR

RENÉE DAHLIA

FOREWORD

Welcome to HIS LORD's SOLDIER, a novella set in 1919 after World War One.

This novella is from my Great War series, and features Rafe, the brother of Luciana (Her Lady's Melody) and James, the brother of Nell (Her Lady's Honor).

If you love gay romance, friends to lovers, and a lot of Christmas dinners, you'll love this novella. It's medium heat with content warnings for war injuries, and polio.

This novella is a finalist in the novella category of the Romance Writers of Australia RuBY (Romantic Book of the Year) Awards in 2022.

If you are keen to keep up to date on new releases and, more importantly, sales, I recommend you sign up to my newsletter at www.reneedahlia.com

I hope you enjoy reading this book!
Renée

ABOUT THE AUTHOR

An avid reader, Renée Dahlia writes contemporary and historical queer romance. Renée is a bisexual cis woman who is fascinated by people and loves to explore human relationships, with a side of humour, through her writing. Renée has a degree in physics and mathematics, using this to write data-based magazine articles for the horse racing industry. Her love of horses often shines through in her fiction, and she loves a good intrigue and to escape the real world in the pages of a book. When she isn't reading or writing, Renée spends her time with her four children, usually watching them play cricket.

HIS LORD'S SOLDIER

Two best friends torn apart by war. Could the re-enactment of four Christmas dinners create a love worth fighting for?

Lord Rafe Stanmore didn't just lose his leg in the war; he lost his charming outlook and all his athletic prowess. His best friend, James St. George, brought him through the worst times with his cheerful letters. Rafe can't bear to face James now he's so altered, but to placate his sister he agrees to a quick visit. His secret longing for James and the nightly relived trauma of the war should be able to stay hidden for a few days.

During the war, James tried to declare his love for Rafe with careful words and extravagant gifts, and never had any indication of his affection being reciprocated. How could gorgeous, athletic, and aristocratic Rafe be interested in polio scarred James? But when Rafe arrives at the farm unexpectedly, James can't resist giving him all the Christmases he missed. It's his last chance to show Rafe exactly how he feels.

Four Christmases to reveal a passion that can't be denied. One last chance to admit the love they've been hiding all along.

CHAPTER ONE

JULY 1919

Rafe leaned all his weight against the post and rail fence, his crutches resting beside him. A light breeze sent the smell of fresh grass floating past and he inhaled deeply. He'd missed being here, at his best friend James' horse farm, although it didn't take a genius to work out why he'd avoided returning for so long. In the parade ring, a wizened up retired jockey led his broodmare, Overby Christmas, along the paved path designed for showcasing horses to their owners. Her weanling colt trotted beside her on long spindly legs, with his ears pricked and his tiny tail held high. Overby Christmas' dark bay coat glistened under the summer sun with dapples across her coat. James had kept her in excellent condition, and Rafe pushed away the cynical annoyance that she wasn't really his horse.

Six years ago, when Rafe had enlisted to fight in the bloody Great War, his best friend gave him a horse. Not just any horse, but a young daughter of the greatest race mare to grace the English turf—Sceptre. Rafe appreciated the expensive gift, but not for the financial gain as most might assume. Any horse would've sufficed because what he truly treasured was the cheerful monthly updates from James about the filly they'd named 'Overby Christmas'. The name started out with hope because everyone said the war would be finished by Christmas, and now the irony of the name summed up his dark view of the whole bloody mess. He should name the colt, 'Not Likely', if it wasn't a bad omen to give a horse such a negative name. His belief in the confident declaration had lasted about as long as it took him to step onto the muddy fields of the Somme.

"Do you think he has a lot of Sceptre in him?" The colt dropped his head to eat some grass. Rafe couldn't believe Overby Christmas was such a beautiful mare. When James had given him the young filly, he'd been uncharacteristically cynical about her. Time, and the war, had changed him until cynicism became his entire outlook. No one, not even his best friend, would give away such a valuable horse unless there was something wrong with her. He'd expected to see a pony size swaybacked crocked legged broodmare, not this glamorous long striding athlete who strode around the parade ring with the swagger that only belonged to those truly confident in their greatness. After six years of reading about this horse, and imagining a pit pony, it was terribly disconcerting to watch a proper racehorse walking before him.

"He's a lot like his sire, Sunstar." James had sent Overby Christmas to the Derby winner because the mating would produce a close relative to Sunstar's Oaks winner Sunny Jane.

Rafe was concerned about Sunstar's own soundness given the horse has reportedly broken down twice during his racing career. He held back a resigned sigh. If James thought it was a good match—and it was on paper—then he wasn't going to argue. James was the expert. And on that note, it was time to clear up something that had bugged him ever since James had gifted him Overby Christmas all those years ago. Rafe didn't glance over at James, just kept his gaze firmly on the end of the beautiful brick stable block that lined the edge of the parade ring.

"I have one question." Now he'd seen the mare, the question grew in statue because the mare was an outstanding type. A proper elegant racehorse with a sloping shoulder and deep girth. "Why would you give away a daughter of Sceptre unless there is something wrong with her?"

"There is nothing wrong with her." James' voice deepened slightly and Rafe turned towards his friend. A faint flush was painted on his cheeks, although the colour could easily be attributed to the wind.

"It's an expensive gift ..."

"...for a very good friend." James breathed in audibly. "Please. Don't worry about the cost. Sceptre lives here on the farm. We look after her for her owner who is a gambler. He offered me Sceptre's next foal in lieu of agistment fees for the remainder of Sceptre's life."

"Aren't you a lucky bastard then?" Sceptre was the only horse to ever win four English Classic races, both the Guineas, the Oaks, and the St Leger, and her first two foals had shown plenty of the same talent, each winning the Cheveley Park Stakes of their year. One of them had already produced the Oaks winner Sunny Jane; hence sending Overby Christmas to Sunny Jane's sire to create a three-quarter sibling—the cavorting colt before them. Sceptre herself had been the most expensive yearling ever sold, thanks to her incredible pedigree, making her own foals virtually impossible to own. There had to be more than luck to it. "James. Seriously, there isn't a more expensive broodmare in all of Europe."

James laughed and the sound washed over his skin, as it always had, awakening the lust he carried with him buried deep in his heart. Rafe had been in love with his best friend forever, but it was one sided. The type of love he wanted wasn't something that could be openly discussed. Oh, he knew James cared for him, as a friend, and the gift of Overby Christmas proved their friendship, nothing more. James couldn't fight and when Rafe had enlisted, this gift gave James something practical to do. It would be silly to attribute anything more to this gesture than the need for James to feel involved with a war he couldn't fight in.

"Her two older sisters are worth much more." James waved to the person leading Overby Christmas and he led the horse towards them. "I know it seems like a lot to give you such a horse. She cost me nothing except to feed her mother, and it's a privilege to have a horse like Sceptre on the farm."

Rafe had no response to that. Before the war, he might have said something happy-go-lucky. He wasn't that person any more.

"I couldn't just give you any horse. Rafe, you are my best friend. I had to give you a horse of consequence to ensure that you would come home from that damned war. It had to matter."

Rafe gritted his teeth, ignoring the weight of emotion in James' voice. "Fat lot of good that did me."

"On the contrary, you are here."

"Not all of me." Rafe muttered under his breath. A soft nose nudged his hip through the fence, and he tried to relax. The foal breathed out, little nostrils fluttering against his pinned up trouser leg.

"Rafe. I'd like to think that my good luck in acquiring Overby Christmas rubbed off on you and now you are here to meet your horses." James didn't mention Rafe's missing leg and Rafe eased out a tight breath. He wasn't ready to have that conversation with James just yet. His whole damned family had encouraged him to visit James to talk about how to navigate the world without a leg. Just because James had polio as a child and had lived for more than twenty years with some paralysis on his left side, didn't at all equip James to understand how Rafe felt. Rafe had always trusted his body, he'd been the fastest runner at school. He'd followed in his father's footsteps and become an amateur champion boxer, and he'd expected to end the war either whole or dead. Not this.

"I'm here." Rafe knew he sounded terse, but he couldn't find it to care anymore.

"Yes. You are." Too much was unsaid between them. James' voice was rough as he said nothing much at all, and yet, there was plenty implied. The war had ended over eight months ago. Rafe's injury had happened two years before that in the autumn of 1916. For a long time after the initial injury,

Rafe had been stuck in a hospital bed fighting off various infections. Not just the amputation site, but also where shrapnel had been imbedded in the rest of his body. No one got their leg blown off cleanly. Eventually, he'd been shipped back to England, and he'd gone home to his parent's estate to recover. To hide from the world and James with his chirpy letters. How on earth could his friend understand the depth of his agony and loss? The Spanish Flu outbreak had provided an additional reason to stay at Stanmore, but the excuses were all gone now and he had to face his best friend's reaction to his new reality. There was only so much begging and pleading he could listen to from everyone before he'd swallowed enough of his pride to get on a train and visit.

James rubbed the mare's head. "Please put them in the number six house paddock." The person holding Overby Christmas nodded and led the broodmare away. The little colt stayed beside Rafe for a few moments, then spun on his heels and galloped after his mother. Rafe wished he could appreciate the spring in the colt's step, the way he lengthened out, like a real racehorse.

"He's a cracking type. We'll wean him soon."

Rafe nodded, not willing to trust his voice. James' letters had kept coming after he'd been injured, and every month he spent a week waiting for the next one. For the sense of normalcy in James' handwriting and his stories from the farm that told of English rural life. The flu had been a terrible blow for Newmarket with many of the township suffering and yet all through that, James found a way to write positive snippets of the world. Horse racing was built on optimism and James had it in spades. There was always something to be excited about, an anticipated foal, a young racehorse who showed promise, an older horse winning after a long layoff with injury.

"You asked me what was wrong with her. Only one thing."

"Oh?" A smugness filled his chest with air. Rafe knew it. The whole story was too good to be true.

"She's unraced."

"Unsound?" There had to be something not right about Overby Christmas—people didn't give away a horse that cost more than the farm she lived on.

James shook his head. "No. It's not her fault. During the war, most racecourses were closed and we had to prioritise which horses we put into training. We didn't have the staff to trial everything either. She's such a beautifully bred filly she didn't need to prove herself on the track. Obviously I would have liked to have tested her, to see if she's the same quality as her older siblings, but there were other priorities."

Rafe ignored James' half-apology about not putting his horse into training. "Most?" If Rafe had thought about it, he would've guessed that all racing would have stopped during the war. He'd been too busy to think about it and damned if he wouldn't feel guilty about that.

"The July Course at Newmarket stayed open and we ran the classics here instead of at Epsom."

"You didn't mention this in your letters."

For the first time since Rafe had arrived at the farm, a frown flashed over James' face. "No. I didn't want you to worry. You had enough to do."

"Why have racing at all?" It was better to ask that, than

7

growl at James for lying to him. He deserved the truth, not happy stories merely told to cheer up Rafe. He wasn't a bloody child who needed to be soothed. Even before he was a soldier, he'd been a boxing champion. He was accustomed to a little blood and gore; had inflicted it on many before he'd paid the price for that. Rafe gripped the fence tighter and let James' soothing voice wash over him, suddenly glad for the normalcy of his tone. Maybe James had it right, and what he had needed was a sugar-coated sweetened version of life back home. It'd given him something to fight for, a reason to keep going when everything seemed impossible.

"We employ a lot of people, Rafe, and we breed a lot of horses. The war needed horses, and the military needed horses. By keeping racing going, it meant we could afford to keep breeding horses for the army."

"Why not just sell to the army?"

James coughed. "Only a moment ago you asked me about Sceptre and the astronomical cost of her progeny. The army pays a pittance compared to the price I can get for a decent young racehorse, let alone one of Overby Christmas' quality. One funds the other, and Newmarket is the best breeding land, so it made sense to give the horse breeders a reason to continue."

"A self-fulfilling prophecy then."

James laughed, a low chuckle under his breath. "God, Rafe, when did you get so cynical?"

"When I was told the war would be over by Christmas, only to spend two damned Christmases in a trench being shot at, and another two in hospital." At least he hadn't been sent to Gallipoli, although that might have been better than the misery of the Somme. Nowhere in war was a good place to be.

"And every time I wrote to you about your horse, her name reminded you of that early hopefulness. I'm sorry."

Rafe shook his head. "It's not your bloody fault. I believed it too. I thought it would be a lark." He didn't need to point out that they'd both obviously been wrong.

"I don't think anyone could have predicted it." James picked up his cane and turned away. "Come on, let's go back to the house and have some lunch."

Rafe nodded and grabbed his crutches. His leg ached from standing on it for so long, and while he wouldn't admit it to his friend, he'd be glad to sit down. Leaning on the fence had helped and having the summer sun warm his skin was also a blessing. Life wasn't all terrible. He could count his blessings; one of them being his best friend James. James may never love him the way Rafe loved James, but it didn't matter. Rafe swung himself along the path, easily keeping pace with James' unsteady gait. The little hitch as he used his hip and his cane to swing his left leg forwards was such a part of James that Rafe suddenly realised he'd missed it. Heat rose up behind his eyes and he blinked hard.

Damn, he was too stoic to cry at such a familiar sight and he wanted to slam that errant thought away. He wasn't sad because James had a limp, he was sad because he'd spent six years away from James. Six years pretending that he didn't miss him all that much. His uneven gait and the odd rhythm of the way he walked hit Rafe in the gut like a surprise punch. He hadn't realised how much he'd missed having James' physical presence beside him. Reading his letters wasn't enough.

It'd been only a fraction of the connection that Rafe craved. He clenched his hands around his crutches, against the urge to run his palm down James' strong spine. In the six years he'd been away, James had broadened with a lot more muscle. In horse terms, James would say that his action hadn't changed but he'd matured and strengthened with age.

James whistled as he opened the passenger door to his car. A border collie leaped into the car and over the seat into the back, nearly knocking Rafe over.

"Sorry. Blue loves riding in the car."

Rafe nodded and tried to sit down without looking like he'd collapsed onto the seat. No amount of exercise had strengthened his leg enough for him to stand on it for any length of time and the lack of progress grated at him. The shrapnel lodged in his knee had festered and for a long time, the doctors had contemplated amputating his other leg too. When it rained, Rafe sometimes wished they had because the pain stabbed at him, and he grumped at everyone around him. It was the other reason he could never let James know how he felt. James deserved to be loved by someone who wasn't going to lash out at random moments; he deserved to be loved by someone who could love completely back again. A wife, most likely, who would give him a family to love. Rafe wasn't sure he could be the person James needed—not with his injuries and ongoing issues—and especially not with the one thing he refused to acknowledge even to himself. Fucking shell shock. It wasn't enough for the war to take his leg and make a mess of the one that remained, the so-called Great War had taken his ability to sleep as well. The engine started with a roar and Rafe tried not to jerk at the sudden noise. James pulled out the crank handle and jumped into the driver's door.

"Are you well? You look very pale."

"Fine. I'm fine."

James nodded, apparently wise enough not to argue with Rafe, and drove the little motorcar back to the main house. The whole way the dog, Blue, panted in his ear. Loud with a slobbery tongue until Rafe wanted to push the creature away. Damn it. He used to love dogs; before he went to war and everything fucking changed.

CHAPTER TWO

After a tense lunch where Rafe didn't speak except for polite nothings like, "Would you pass the salt, please?" James fled to his office to do paperwork; or just lick his wounds. Blue lay sleeping in front of the fireplace, a picture of relaxation. James wished his heart would stop pounding and his muscles could relax like that. He'd been so overwhelmed when he'd read the telegram stating Rafe would visit that he hadn't been able to collect him from the station. Finally, six long years after Rafe had left, James would see him again, and he'd almost panted like Blue after a long run at the thought.

To avoid an embarrassing scene in public, he'd sent his farm manager in the horse truck and everything had gone downhill from there. Rafe had stepped out of the truck and James hadn't been able to hold back the gasp. Of course, he knew Rafe would be different. He knew he'd lost his leg nearly three years previous and had spent months in a military hospital before being sent home to England. From there, Rafe had stayed at his family estate and James should've visited. His parents had spent months visiting and had reported back about Rafe. Now all of James' excuses seemed flimsy. This differences only began with Rafe's leg. Rafe's face was lined with a permanent frown on his brow and deep wrinkles around his eyes, and his dark brown hair had turned silver around the temples. A nasty scar ran down one cheek and James glimpsed an angry red scar on the back of his left hand. Obviously the injury had affected more than just his leg. But the biggest change, and the one that stabbed James in the heart, was Rafe's demeanour. Gone was his charming competitive friend who teased him with joyful laughter, replaced by a gruff man who growled under his breath.

"What do I do now?" James muttered to himself.

"Sell him." Rafe's deep voice—deeper than it used to be, surely—rang around the room and James startled, immediately sitting bolt upright.

"Excuse me?"

"I assume you mean the colt. Sell him."

James shrugged, aiming for casual and ending up somewhere awkward instead. "If that's what you want. He's yours."

"And yours."

James half-stood, his chest tightening, a vice of his own creation. "Would you stop arguing with me about Overby Christmas? She is a gift. Yours to do with as you please."

"I'm not arguing about the mare."

"You aren't?" James swayed slightly and sat down again.

"No. I read your letters, James." Rafe made it sound threatening. James' body didn't hear it that way. His chest swelled because Rafe had read his letters. "I recall that you paid the service fee on the colt, and that makes him half yours. We should sell him and split the profit evenly, as you would any other horse you owned in partnership."

James' skin prickled at the idea of being in partnership with Rafe. It was what he wanted more than anything else in the world. For the last six years, once a month, James had written a letter to his best friend Rafe. It'd been tempting to write more often and every single letter, he ended with "*I love you with all of my heart. Please come home to me.*" And then he rewrote every letter in neater script without the incriminating last sentence, never telling Rafe how he felt. Those first drafts would never be found because he burned them. He would never risk them being found because he didn't just love Rafe as a friend, he truly loved him. Always had; and that type of love wasn't legal. He knew other couples—like his sister Nell and her Beatrice—who loved like he did and lived good lives without the law getting involved, but it took dedication and care and trust to stay safe. All things that needed to be discussed and negotiated with the other person, and James... well... he wasn't brave enough to admit his love to Rafe. Instead, once a month, his ritual had been to craft a letter to Rafe about his horse. A horse who was far too expensive to give away, because of course the gift was a sloppy attempt to show his true feelings. The hardest part was getting approval from his father, who still owned the farm. James was merely the manager; making all the decisions so his parents could retire. They spent most of their time travelling to visit friends now, and being a sentimental fool, he kept all their telegrams from their travels. If Rafe had ever sent a reply to one of his letters, he probably would've framed it, or kept it under his pillow.

"That is logical. We will prepare him for Tattersalls."

Now Rafe was here, on his farm, and it hadn't gone quite as James had planned. He knew about Rafe's leg and to be honest, he didn't give a flying fuck about it. No, that wasn't true; deep down inside he had to admit that a tiny part of him was glad. Rafe had always been so athletic—a boxing champion like his father, a fast runner, a brilliant horse rider who could make an ordinary horse lift and become special—and now Rafe was... more in the same welterweight class as James. Even as he thought it, he cursed himself. It wasn't fair to think that, let alone want that; but since when was life fair? It wasn't fair that he'd caught bloody polio when was he was five either.

"And you will bill me for half the cost of getting him ready for sale." Rafe paused and his dark brown eyes narrowed. James couldn't tell the colour of his eyes from this far away, but he'd known Rafe his whole life and eye colour surely didn't change during a war. It had to be the one constant—Rafe's brown eyes that reminded him of the dapples on a dark bay racehorse. Healthy, shining, and ready for action.

"As you wish." James was momentarily impressed that his voice didn't tremble with the need coursing through his veins. He was glad to be seated, where his desk hid the obvious sign of his attraction to Rafe.

"And..." Rafe paused for a moment and James gulped. "You will also send me the bill for six years of care for Overby Christmas and for half of the costs for the colt so far."

James tried not to breath out in relief as Rafe accepted his gift. "Those have been sent every month to Stanmore, except for the first year which was part of my gift."

"Paid by my father?"

"By the family estate, I assume."

Rafe nodded. Before the war, he would've made some dismissive joke about grabbing from his inheritance. This version of Rafe where he kept everything close and didn't joke or share was unsettling. James wanted to shove his hands in his pockets or thump his cane on the floor. Whenever he was stressed, he walked through the paddocks on the farm and used his cane to eradicate thistles. The lower weanling paddock could do with a good whacking.

"Is there a problem?" Rafe asked.

"No. How is your room?"

"Very comfortable. Thank you."

James thumped his cane. "Damn it, Rafe." Blue raised his head for a half-second, then went back to sleep. Rafe stiffened, still standing at the edge of the room, then slowly raised his eyebrows but again, he didn't speak.

"How long have we been friends?"

"Since birth." Rafe was three years older than James but it had never mattered. Ever since they could both walk, they'd chased each other around the lawns on their respective parents' properties until James couldn't run anymore. His limp hadn't stopped their friendship, it'd brought them closer because Rafe had never pitied James. He'd always challenged him—just enough—not to hurt him but with respect for his abilities. Rafe's mother, Lady Stanmore, had gone to medical school in Amsterdam with James' mother, Lady St.

George. Thankfully, his parents had never pushed him into higher education, just because they had done it, and had set up the farm under his management as soon as he'd shown an ability as a good judge of horseflesh. A love of racehorses ran in the family. This farm, Braemount Stud, had been purchased by his grandfather who wanted a Newmarket property for his horses, and named after a mountain near the family estate in Scotland. His father had improved the stock since taking over before James was born. The old Duke hadn't been content with using the family lands to breed racehorses. It was sheep country up there and he'd needed to have the best, so he'd bought the farm from someone down on their luck. A nice parallel to his own purchase of Overby Christmas.

"And here we are. Being polite and talking about money." James heard the whine in his tone and swallowed. The current Duke was James' uncle who had little interest in the horse farm and had sold it to James' father, the Duke's younger brother, decades ago. One day, James would gift the farm in his will to one of his nephews or nieces. He had known for years he would never have children of his own, although a recent letter from his sister opened up the possibility of adoption. Nell's lover Beatrice had a brother with an interest in horses. If the young boy came up to scratch, he might be a good person to gift the farm to one day.

"We can't go back, James." Rafe sat down in a chair and tucked his crutches beside him, as if the act of him moving would remind James of the bloody obvious.

With James caught up planning the future, he had to play catch up, and it took a few breaths before he could find his voice. "No one can go back. Forgive me for missing my friend."

Rafe shook his head, an infinitesimal movement, barely there at all. "I'm not the same person as I was." There was an anguish in Rafe's voice and James wished he'd been more open with his friend. He wanted to charge across the room and wrap Rafe in a hug to reassure him it didn't matter. He loved him anyway.

"I don't give a rats arse about your missing leg, Rafe. You know me, you know..." About his polio and his own struggles.

"It's not that. Inside, James. I'm not the same person. How could I be? The things I've seen. The things I've done..." Rafe buried his head in his hands and James' breath burned in his throat. There was no chance he might ever understand what being a soldier was like, nor the impact it might have on someone. He hadn't even bothered to enlist, knowing he'd be rejected by the army. But he'd been useful during the war, nonetheless, breeding sound, strong horses for them. None of that eliminated his level of care, or the depth of his empathy. James wished, more than anything, that he could've been there, beside Rafe to support him, to hold his hand as he healed, and yet, he'd been too scared to go to him when he'd first arrived back in England. No gift would ever make up for James' choice not to be brave.

A long silence descended on the room, so long that the shadows changed. It was summer, the sun wouldn't set for hours, yet at this time of the afternoon, James could mark the changing hour by the shadow cast by the giant oak tree, visible out the window as it stood guard over the house paddock. His life hadn't changed during the war, broodmares were mated, foals were born, young horses broken in. The worst inconvenience had been the reduced racing program and having to sell good quality horses to the Army.

"One thing never changes, and that's the quality of my uncle's whisky. Would you like some?" James walked over to the cabinet and poured two decent helpings of the fifteen-year aged whisky. He carried one tumbler over to Rafe and placed it on the side table beside him. Years ago, he'd learned never to touch Rafe because whenever their skin brushed, it released a spark like a crack of lightning. It was no excuse, but it was the reason he'd been too scared to go to Rafe. If he'd gone to his sick-bed, everyone would know how he felt. There'd be no hiding from it, and if Rafe didn't feel the same way, James had no idea how he would go on.

"Those were the days. When all of Mother's friends would gather for Christmas, and your uncle would open a bottle he'd saved for the day." Rafe's voice had a whimsical note and James wanted to capture it and put it in a locket to carry against his heart.

"It's pretty handy having a Scottish distillery in the family." His uncle, the Duke of Tulloch, had also been rather handy in the fight to keep racing going during the war. It was good for the morale of the people, and James had been proved correct in the end. The public adoration when Lady Douglas' Gainsborough won the Derby last year was worth the fight to keep racing; it had given everyone hope in the summer as the war dragged on, and when the war ended, James couldn't help but see Gainsborough's victory as the joy that pulled England through to victory in the war.

"What year is this one?" Rafe sipped the whisky. A droplet clung to his lips as he lowered the glass, and James wanted to lick it off.

"It's a 1900 version."

"I was twelve and so damned keen to be an adult. Why did no one tell us it would be like this?"

James grinned as the little hint of the old Rafe charm almost appeared. He'd idolised Rafe back then, when he'd been only nine, unable to follow him around, but hovering nearby whenever he could.

"All responsibility and no joy?" James took a guess, one that didn't reflect his own reality.

"Something like that." Rafe mumbled into his tumbler and after taking another sip, he leaned his head back and closed his eyes. James squeezed his own eyes shut tight. Otherwise he was going to salivate over that long column of Rafe's exposed throat, so perfect for kissing, with a hint of stubble across his jaw. The texture would be perfect on his lips. He swallowed. If Rafe wanted to be taken back to more joyful times, James could create that for him. He could capture the moments Rafe reminisced about. Lightness filled his body as the practical solution began to appear in his mind. Never mind that it was mid-summer. He would recreate every Christmas dinner that Rafe had missed during the war. Perhaps not with rationing, although on the farm, they'd been lucky to grow all their own produce and hadn't missed much. Flour had been difficult to come by on occasion, and for one memorable month, they'd ground the horse's cornmeal into flour and used recipes his parents had discovered on their travels to South America. He could even recreate that into a meal; or rather Cook could. He picked up his pen and started to scribble some plans on a scrap of paper.

"Some things never change." Rafe interrupted his writing.

"Oh?"

"You look exactly how I remembered you. Always hunched over your desk, scribbling away on a piece of paper. Did you look like this when you wrote me all the happy tales from Newmarket?" Rafe's voice had that flirtatious note of old. James kept on writing, with his face turned away from Rafe so he wouldn't see the flush on his cheeks. He wrote nonsensical things, like the list of Derby winners during the war. Durbar, Pommern, Fifinella, Gay Crusader, and of course, the incredible Gainsborough.

"My favourite story was the one about how you sold two colts to Lord Brackenstone after the Derby in 1915."

James barked out a laugh. "Pommern's Derby. The poor horse being named after a German."

"Presumably he was named prior to the war?"

James nodded. "Yes, the owner has been very overt about the fact that he named him in 1913 as a yearling. No one cares about the truth though, because a German battleship with the same name was destroyed by our fleet about a month after Pommern won the Derby."

Rafe smiled. "Blast. That's an unfortunate coincidence."

"Selling those two colts to Brackenstone on the evening after Pommern's Derby has to be one of the most satisfying sales I've ever made. It was during the post-Derby function that I made the sale, and then to get the telegraph a week after I delivered them to his estate. *It appears I got drunk and purchased two colts from you. Stop.*"

"Something of a surprise for the old man." Rafe's tone softened as if he were smiling.

"He's not that old, but he is a crafty one..." James paused, unwilling to admit he'd once been sucked in by Brackenstone's wiles. They'd slept together once a long time ago—a mediocre experience—and Brackenstone had been trying to get a repeat ever since. "... it was nice to get one back over him."

"Not crafty enough not to get drunk in the presence of a horse salesman! Please tell me they were slow."

James chuckled. "Would I sell a slow horse intentionally? I mean, they weren't Derby quality, but each of them won a couple of minor races, so I'm sure Brackenstone had a bit of fun with them as he posed in the winner's circles. The Minoru colt, Minimum Pounds, ended up winning four races and the other one, Legs Eleven, become a fairly good chaser and won a few over sticks too. Brackenstone would've made a decent pile of cash when Legs Eleven won his first steeplechase. He paid well over the odds at thirty to one."

"He's not the gambler who owns Sceptre?"

James shook his head. "No. Not many are in the same realm as Sceptre's owner." Brackenstone gambled with men's bodies, not money. He was well known in racing circles for a new affair every flat season, often with men not from the peerage. Had Rafe heard the rumours? James had been very careful not to have his name too closely associated with Brackenstone after their sole encounter.

James stood up. "I'm sorry. I need to go and talk to the cook about dinner." He had a sudden urge to get away from this conversation before he admitted his inclinations in front of Rafe. The risk that Rafe might discard their entire friend-ship if he knew about James wasn't a bet he was willing to take. It was better to be friends with him and never kiss him, than to never have him in his life. War had changed Rafe and it may have made him more judgemental. An outsider's chance, but even those won occasionally.

CHAPTER THREE

R afe didn't mind the silence as he sat down to dinner a couple of nights later. He'd avoided James for a day or two, under the pretence of needing to recover from his travels. The trip from Stanmore had been quite wearing, as he'd first taken the train down to London to see his sister Luciana who'd just returned from the war. One night there staying with friends was enough for him. It'd been wonderful to see Luciana; she was one of the few people who understood what he'd been through. Luciana and his mother had worked as doctors at the front, but it wasn't just that which meant Luciana understood him. They'd had a rather open conversation about love, a decent distraction from the usual questions about his injuries. Their friend's house in London had only served to give him reminders of the war until all he'd wanted was to get away to the one place the war hadn't touched.

Between that and the discussion with Luciana, he'd sent James a telegram and had nervously boarded the train to Newmarket. To Braemount Stud and James. Unrequited desire was never relaxing, however, these last couple of days had started to settle him. He could stay here for a month or so until the chemistry that flickered around James became too overwhelming and he'd need to flee again. If he kept to himself, he might find some sort of temporary peace.

In the dining room, James hovered awkwardly, which was quite the achievement given he was seated on the other end of the small table. Rafe had a foreboding sense that James wanted something from him, and Rafe wasn't sure he could give it. Whatever it was.

"Tell me. What was Christmas like in 1914?" James asked. For the first time since sitting down, Rafe noticed the table was decorated rather like Christmas with the napkin folded rather like a Christmas tree. The centre of the table was covered with conifer branches, and elegant candle holders had holly woven around them.

"You don't want to know about that." He'd been caught up in heavy fire and his entire cavalry unit had been forced to retreat. It wasn't the best beginning to the war, although he remembered feeling invincible as he galloped away from the machine gun fire with his horse twisting and turning as they dodged trees in the forest. Back when the forests were still there before they'd been obliterated by years of heavy shelling.

"I do." James paused, presumably waiting for Rafe to answer but he didn't know how. How does one describe the miserable weather and the exhilaration of escape?

"Would you like to know what I did?" James asked.

Rafe glanced up. "I read your letters, James. I know what you did."

"Every single day I would read the Roll of Honour in the newspapers."

Rafe tried not to growl. Better that than listen to the thud in his chest at the thought of James scanning the papers every day for the names of his friends and relatives. "Honour?"

"That's what they called the casualties list. First it had the list of Killed in Action, sorted by surname, then Died of Wounds, then Died Other Causes, then..."

"Stop. I don't need to be reminded of all of that." Fucking hell. He'd seen people die. It wasn't at all the same as reading a sanitised list of their names while sitting in a plush lounge surrounded by all the trappings of Christmas.

James' face reddened. "I'm sorry. Yesterday you told me you weren't a child and you didn't want to happy version. What I wrote in my letters was the happy version of life here. I didn't tell you about the—"

Rafe did growl this time. He hadn't expected a casual comment to hold such weight with James. "—It wasn't a criticism of your letters." He hauled in a deep breath and began the sanitised version. Two could play at that game. "In 1914, I was a member of a Cavalry Corp as part of the British Expeditionary Force. And, no, I wasn't part of the Great Christmas Truce." He would never comprehend why everything at war needed to be labelled great. There wasn't much great about mucking around in the mud being shot at.

"Oh, I read about that."

"The mud?" Rafe growled, his shoulders tense and his stomach heavy.

James chuckled. "The Christmas Truce. The papers on Boxing Day were full of hope and glory about it. How our troops were gracious as they swapped tobacco with the enemy, while the Germans lit candles and sang songs."

"Nothing like that happened where I was." It'd been bitterly cold and he'd spent the evening huddled against his horse, trying to keep warm as a light snow fell, after having escaped with his life. Charlie had been a good horse. A prick of heat stabbed from behind his eyes—Charlie hadn't survived past New Year. He'd gone through seven different horses in France, before finally ending up in hospital himself. After the first three, Charlie, Joe, and Triumph, he'd stopped naming them. Whoever had named Triumph had it all wrong, and he wasn't going to jinx another horse with a name like that.

"Can I ask where you were?"

"No." Rafe automatically spat out a clipped response, then realised it didn't matter anymore. "Sorry. Habit. I can probably tell you now that the war is finished. We, that is, my calvary unit, were in the process of withdrawing after the Battle of Messines. That's south of Ypres. After that we ended up involved in the Battle of Arras and fought all through Christmas and New Year. It was bloody cold."

James suddenly stood up, his chair scraping on the wooden floor. "This isn't going how I planned."

"What exactly have you planned?" Rafe fiddled with the napkin on his plate, undoing the pleats that made it into a tree shape.

"I wanted to give you the Christmas dinners you'd missed while you were away, but I didn't intend to interrogate you about your time over there. I wanted this to be happy, even though you stated you didn't want happy." James mumbled and ran his hand through his hair. Rafe tried not to think about how James' hair would feel if it were his fingers threading through the short brown hair. When James coughed, Rafe realised he'd been staring at him without answering.

"I'd be amenable to such a plan." The concept, enjoying all the Christmas dinners he'd missed, was rather nice and filled Rafe's throat with a lump, not dissimilar to having eaten an overly large mouthful of Christmas pudding. Rich and sweet and decadent.

"Excellent." James made his way over to the bell-pull. A moment later, even before James was seated once more, a footman entered the room. "Stewart. You may begin to serve dinner."

Stewart bowed low and left. Rafe's family hardly ever sat down to formal dinners with all the manners and whatnot, but he supposed if this was to be Christmas, then he'd better try and remember how to behave.

"I might have worn a tie if I known it would be Christmas dinner." His joke fell a little flat, although James did blush rather prettily. "I meant it as a jest, not a criticism. I am thankful for this idea of yours."

James opened his mouth as if to speak, but pinched his lips closed when Stewart entered the room pushing a trolley laden with silver dishes. Stewart transferred the food to the table, removing the shining lids and the room filled with the warm scent of mushroom soup. His favourite.

"Would you like me to serve?"

"No. I think we can manage ourselves. Thank you."

Stewart bowed his head. "Ring the bell when you are

ready for the next course." He trundled out of the room with the trolley.

"Shall I serve?" James asked, already on his feet. "Please, you are my guest."

Rafe nodded. Last Christmas, he'd been at Stanmore, surrounded by most of his family. Only his sister, Luciana, wasn't there as she was still at Ypres working as a doctor in a field hospital. His other sister, Carolyn and her husband and their three young children attended, along with his parents and his youngest brother Peter. The noise had been over-whelming, and he'd retired early. To sit here with James, just the two of them, and celebrate at the wrong time of year over a quiet dinner would have been very pleasant if it wasn't for the crackle of lust in Rafe's veins. Every time James reached out in friendship and did something nice for Rafe, he wished he could enjoy it fully without this incessant need to pretend that straightforward friendship was all that he felt.

"Here you go." James handed him a bowl of soup, then added a small plate at the side of his soup. The plate had a slice of tart, with crispy brown crust and a delicious looking cheesy filling with little bubbles of melted cheese on the top. Rafe's mouth moistened as wholesome scents surrounded him.

"By God, I missed good food."

"In the war?"

"No. When I was a child. Of course, in the war." Rafe kept his gaze on his soup, regretful of his harsh tone. James was his friend and he was trying his damnedest. He didn't need Rafe's surly tongue lashing. "At first, the supply chain worked well and we ate a reasonable diet, but as the war went on, it was bully beef and hard tack."

"I'm sorry."

Rafe glared at his friend. "It's not your fucking fault." He breathed in quickly. "My apologies."

Laughter filled the room. "Rafe. I work on a horse farm. I've used that word before. We've said that word with each other before."

Fucking. Erotic images filled Rafe's vision, and the saliva in his mouth increased until he had to swallow awkwardly. Yes, he had imagined fucking James many a time. He could picture James' naked spine underneath him, the roundness of his arse, and the tilt of his head as Rafe entered him. Rafe's pulse galloped like a bolting horse, completely out of control, head thrown high, and tongue over the bit.

"Are you well?"

Rafe gripped his spoon tighter, as sweat dripped down his spine. "Very well, thank you."

"You look rather flushed."

"I'm fine." Rafe needed to eat some soup before he ruined their friendship forever by kissing James. "Please sit down and we can enjoy this food."

James nodded, served himself, and did as Rafe asked. Fuck—he really didn't need to think about James' obedience to his growled command. When Rafe looked up, James' face was bright red. If Rafe didn't know better, he would've assumed James knew exactly what he was thinking and wanted the same thing. Unfortunately, that was merely a dream and the best he could do would be to enjoy the soup.

James couldn't possibly eat while Rafe stared at him like that. If he didn't know better, he'd assume Rafe was imagining him naked. He cursed his overactive imagination. They'd been friends since they were babies—if Rafe had any inclination towards men, he would've known about it. There had never been a rumour about Rafe, not in London where those things were spoken about in hushed whispers, and not in their extended family and friend's network. Rafe's parents and his had been friends for as long as he could remember, and their other good friends, the Howicks, were closely related to Lord Dalhinge who had a male lover. He hadn't escaped the rumour mill himself. Those who'd been around Newmarket for long enough would remember the gossip of Tagalie's Derby year, after he'd slept with Lord Brackenstone. Bloody rumours. He'd been too young—only 21—and had used Brackenstone to explore his own inclinations. Brackenstone had a reputation for spending time with men, and James had assumed he could learn from him without risking mentioning his desires to someone unknown. The disappointment had faded over time. Other affairs helped with that. He'd rather think of the horse than Brackenstone.

Tagalie was a petite grey filly, one of the very few to have won a Derby. Her win coincided with James' father, Lord St. George, taking him aside and reminding him of to be careful. Father had heard Brackenstone boasting of the conquest and James' stomach sank at the memory of how bloody naïve he'd been. Thank God his father hadn't blinked an eye at learning of his only son's inclinations. He knew how lucky he was to have a father who'd been a spy in his youth and had seen everything; had probably done everything with everyone if the truth were known.

"Don't you like mushroom soup?" Rafe asked. James schooled his expression as he glanced up from the as yet untouched bowl of soup.

"Sorry, I was lost in thought."

"And I assumed the distasteful expression was the soup. Why order it for dinner if you don't like it?"

The knot in James' stomach loosened at Rafe's quiet jest. "I ordered it for you. It used to be your favourite."

Rafe's eyes widened slightly. "You remember?"

James held his breath for a second so he didn't blurt out that he remembered everything about Rafe, storing up little pieces of knowledge about him like a squirrel hoarding for the winter. "Yes. You are my best friend. Of course, I remember which soup you prefer."

"I am also partial to curried pumpkin."

"I know. The cook has had excellent recipe that she learned from the cook at Lord Dalhinge's estate."

Rafe smiled, for the first time in the day, or so it seemed. "How is Lord Dalhinge? And Will Carlingford? I spent the night at Ashwin's London house prior to coming here but they were in the country."

"Still bickering." James grinned back at Rafe. Having Sanjay and Will in their lives was such a blessing. He'd never had to question his own inclinations because he'd grown up with the two of them in their social circle.

Rafe's shoulders visibly relaxed. "That's excellent to hear.

I was unfortunately too preoccupied to ask after them when in London."

Preoccupied with what, James wanted to ask, but he was enjoying Rafe's current mood and didn't want to ruin it. "We are so lucky."

One eyebrow on Rafe's brow raised up slowly. So slowly. "How's that?" It dawned on James that his comment wouldn't be well received in the context of Rafe's war injury.

"To be surrounded by so much love. Your parents, mine, the Howicks, and of course Sanjay and Will."

Rafe's expression softened. "Yes, from that perspective. We are very lucky. I doubt I'll ever be so fortunate."

"You are a great catch." James almost slipped up and admitted his love. Unless Rafe shared his inclinations, James would not be as fortunate as Sanjay and Will either. But he would never risk his friendship with Rafe, and to hide the chill that rushed across his neck, he jumped up and pulled the bell-pull.

"Are you keen for the next course?"

James forced himself not to spin around guiltily. "It's roast goose. My favourite."

"Does that mean you will rush my favourite to get to yours?" Rafe grinned and James' spine relaxed. He sat down and deliberately ate the soup without breaking eye contact with Rafe. Heat blossomed between them, virtually crackling across the table, like a winter storm building in the sky with lightning about to be unleashed. If James touched Rafe, he knew it would crackle and burn, as if the lightning had hit a tree with a sharp crack. He didn't even taste the mushroom soup as he ate, he was so focused on Rafe's attentive gaze. It wasn't until Stewart opened the door that he dropped his gaze away from Rafe. A chill spread slowly over his skin. He'd never been so open about his desire for Rafe as now. What if he'd made a giant mistake?

"Merry un-Christmas. Tonight we have roast goose with Yorkshire puddings, fresh beans from the farm's kitchen gardens, roast potatoes, and of course, Cook's famous gravy."

"Thank you, Stewart."

"Please send my compliments to Cook. The soup was excellent." Rafe's solid manners helped banish the nervous way James' stomach flipped. Stewart transferred the dishes to the table and lifted off the silver lids. The smell of roast goose, so rich and succulent, filled the room and James breathed it deep into his lungs.

"Shall I serve?"

"Yes please, Stewart," James said. They'd eaten goose at Lord Dalhinge's estate for Christmas in 1914 but his favourite dish had been marred by those who weren't there. His mother was an only child, and she'd basically adopted her two best friends into the role of aunty. On his father's side, his uncle, the Duke of Tulloch, had four children all around his age but Scotland was far away, and they only came to Newmarket for Christmas every few years. One year up there, one year in Newmarket, and one year to spend with his mother's created family. Until the Christmas of 1914 he'd thought it was a bit much to have Christmas with them all, but with so many of them away that year, he'd suddenly realised the beauty of his mother's created family of friends because he missed them with an ache in his chest.

"We ate this identical meal on the first Christmas you

were away. We all still thought the war would be over quickly." James paused, waiting for the Overby Christmas joke but
it didn't come. Not even a comment about the soup; he
couldn't remember what type of soup they'd had that day and
had just substituted Rafe's favourite for tonight. "It was
surprisingly normal; except that half our friends were away."
James' sister, Nell, had joined up as a veterinarian, while
Rafe's mother Marie, and his sister Luciana, were working as
doctors. Of course, Rafe had joined the cavalry and had taken
one of James' best geldings, Charles of Arrott, as a mount,
while Ashwin ran his family's shipyard to help the war effort
that way. Well, James had bred many a good horse for the
calvary, so he shouldn't feel like he'd contributed nothing.
Back at that first Christmas of the war, his achievements had
felt insignificant compared to others. Distant. James waited as
Stewart carved the goose and plated up some for Rafe before
serving him.

Stewart fiddled about with the dishes for a few more
minutes. "More wine?"

"No thank you. We can serve ourselves."

Stewart bowed and left the room. His duties around the
house didn't often extend to formal dinner duties, although
they did hold a dinner function for Guineas week every May
for all their owners and other distinguished racing guests and
Stewart was an integral part of planning and running that
event.

"Nothing was normal about that year." Rafe's expression
became grimmer than usual. Over the past few days, James
had become accustomed to this version of Rafe—gone was
the charmer, replaced by a darker expression.

"No, I suppose not." James needed to change the subject towards happier things to keep this meal as he'd planned, a celebration. "Remember the little goat cart we used to have?"

Rafe's eyes lit up and he almost grinned, loosening the twist in James' stomach. "Do you still have that? Who had the wild idea to hitch a couple of goats to a small cart and try and drive them around the farm?"

James was pretty sure it was Nell's idea, although she'd blamed him afterwards. "Goats aren't the most trainable of creatures. Smart though."

"Too bloody smart! Remember that time you finally managed to get them both going in a straight line together and Nell and Ashwin jumped out of the hedge yelling Surprise!"

James laughed. "Bloody tipped me out on my backside. And all I could hear was you cursing at my sister, and Ashwin running down the driveway chasing the goats."

"You're right, you know. We have been so bloody lucky to grow up like this." An odd expression passed over Rafe's face before he picked up his cutlery and started to eat his dinner. James tipped some gravy over the slice of roast goose and cut off a small piece. When he put it in his mouth, flavour exploded on his tongue. The crisp salty skin, the succulent flesh, the rich gravy, and all with a hint of garlic and thyme. Delicious.

"Would you like more wine?" Rafe asked.

"Yes. It's fine. I'll pour. You don't need to get up."

Rafe frowned. "I can manage." His growl reminded James of all the times people assumed he was helpless, and he nodded jerkily.

"Thank you. More wine would be marvellous." He focused on eating to give Rafe the time and space he needed to navigate standing on one leg and pouring wine for them. If it'd been him, he would've hated to be stared at, so he tried his best to ignore Rafe. An impossible task, given the way his body virtually vibrated whenever Rafe was near. Naturally, Rafe didn't require his crutches for balance, and the reminder of Rafe's previous athletic feats warmed James as if someone had spilled a mug of mulled wine against his chest. Initially pleasantly warm with a wonderful perfume, but quickly unpleasant. He was sure Rafe wouldn't appreciate the comparison to his pre-war physique, and if James was honest, he was increasingly angry with himself for the way his joy at having Rafe nearby was tinged with a bit of relief. Before the war, he'd always been a tiny bit envious of Rafe. Not in an awful way, but simply in awe of him because Rafe was so incredibly physical when he wasn't. It wasn't the comparison so much as the idea that he wasn't enough for someone like Rafe who had everything. Incredibly handsome, physically gifted and strong, and charming to boot.

His friend of old barely existed anymore; although his more rugged features and the silver hair at his temples somehow made him more handsome. More virile. Was it really envy James felt deep in the twists of his gut, or something else completely? He couldn't work it out, and maybe it was merely a confusing shift in the way they viewed each other. The most confusing part for James was the shift in Rafe's personality. He'd fallen in love with the charmer. Rafe always had a smile for everyone, a quick witted joke to set people at ease, and James adored it when that charm was aimed at him. For those brief moments, James had been the centre of Rafe's world and it was everything—everything—he'd ever desired. He gulped down his wine, tasting the rich red Burgundy full of tannins with a hint of blackberry on his tongue, and realised that perhaps he was in love with pre-war Rafe. Maybe he wasn't in love with the Rafe who sat in this room with him and ate his food. Was it wrong to grief for a lost love when the person in question was right there with him? When his love had never been acknowledged or reciprocated? James wanted to whack his cane against some thistles. He was a terrible person for thinking like this.

CHAPTER FOUR

"Fuck. Bollocks." Rafe's fingers refused to push the bloody pin through his trousers, and he nearly threw the blasted thing across the room. He would persist with the damned thing because he'd tried moving around on crutches without pinning up the empty pant leg and it'd been a damned hindrance. Being able to swear aloud felt fucking great though. Almost like being a real soldier again.

"Fucking fuck. Damn and blast and goddamn it. Piss and shit and goggle-eyed tit." He wasn't going to get reprimanded by his commanding officer either. Swearing wasn't allowed in the army unless a soldier was under duress—which was most of the fucking time when being shelled constantly. At first, he'd laughed at the way everyone tried not to say bugger and instead went with booger as if that made any difference, but in the end he hadn't cared that the word often used to describe him was used as a swearword. Whatever got men through this fucking mess was fine by him. And when one of them jerked him off with an apology for wanting him, he'd only wished they'd be free to be themselves. What was the point of war otherwise? A loud knock at the door made him drop the pin and it bounced on the wooden floor, ending up out of his reach. Typical of his luck.

"Yes?"

"It's James. Can I come in?"

Rafe automatically stood up, not wanting James to see him sitting on the bed arguing with his bloody pants. "Enter."

James stepped through the door with a smug little grin on his face. Rafe wasn't sure if he wanted to punch it off or kiss him until he groaned. Damn it; the thought of kissing James sent blood rushing to his cock. He sat down before his erection became obvious. At least the bloody explosion that fucked his legs had hit him lower down and he was still capable of fucking. Some mercy out of all this, except the one person he really wanted to touch was out of reach. In the room with him, but unavailable.

"Can I help?"

With the erection—absolutely. Rafe coughed, glad no one could hear his thoughts. "I dropped the damned pin for my pants. Can you grab it?"

"I wondered why you were late for dinner. Is it over there?" James pointed, and Rafe shook his head and pointed to the location of the pin. James bent over, arse in the air, to grab the pin. Fuck, bugger, and blast. He wanted to grab that view with both hands and run his tongue over James' skin. His own skin blazed with heat and he tried to think of... No, all his brain supplied was, "lay back and think of England" which was no fucking assistance.

"Ahh, here it is. Shall I?" James spun around and knelt on the floor in front of Rafe. Close enough for his breath to graze over Rafe's hard cock. If he tilted his hips a little bit, he'd almost be able to touch James' mouth. His arm muscles started to shake with holding himself still. James pinned up the empty pants leg with ease, apparently unaware of the agony coursing through Rafe's body. When he glanced up, still kneeling on the ground, and stared wide-eyed and rosy cheeked at Rafe, it took everything in him not to thread his hands through James' hair and pull him closer.

"Thank you." Rafe hated the way his voice gave him away, hoarse with desire.

James stood up and stepped away. "My pleasure." It was just the polite thing that everyone said, it didn't mean anything. Try telling that to Rafe's body. His damned veins were going to overheat at this rate; they'd explode like a shell and rain shards of metallic pain down on him. James picked up Rafe's crutches and laid them on the bed beside him, as if completely unaware of Rafe's state. Thankfully.

"Come on. Dinner will be getting cool." James walked out of the room, closing the door with a slight bang, leaving Rafe alone with his embarrassing desire. Oh, he wasn't embarrassed about wanting to fuck James. But he was ashamed of his lack of control. He rolled across the bed and grabbed a handkerchief from the drawer in the bedside table. With quick hands, he undid the fly of his pants, wrapped his cock in silk, and quickly stroked himself to completion. The release came faster and harder than usual, and he lay back on the bed in a sated dose. Not for too long; because like James had said, he was late for dinner.

James fled to the dining room, his face on fire. He couldn't believe he'd knelt before Rafe like that, as if he was willing to submit to Rafe's commands. Oh, he was. Absolutely willing and ready. That act ranked highly among his most wanted desires. It wouldn't have taken much to open Rafe's pants and wrap his lips around Rafe's cock. The earlier doubt over his love for Rafe fled; Rafe was the one he wanted. The one he'd always wanted and no complex thoughts about worth would ever change that. James would prove he was worthy of Rafe.

Of course, as he'd pinned the pants leg, he'd noticed the size of Rafe's cock. Was it hard for him? No, that was too much to hope for. Probably Rafe had just finished touching himself; he was a very masculine man who would need frequent... James needed to stop thinking like this before he spilled in his own pants and became unfit to attend dinner. He hoped Rafe hadn't noticed the way his hand had slipped on the metal pin, his fingers slightly damp. He opened the door to the dining room and rushed to the side board; his cane thumping on the wooden floor. With shaky fingers, he poured himself a nip of whisky. He swallowed it down, relishing the burn on his throat. The familiar taste helped settle him and after a few long breaths he was ready to eat dinner with Rafe. Two nights ago, they'd had the 1914 Christmas dinner re-enactment. He'd kept himself busy in the intervening time—there was always plenty to do on the farm in summer. Tonight was 1915—Pommern's Derby year. He hoped Rafe wouldn't ask more questions about Lord Brackenstone. Imagining that conversation was a sure-fire way of removing the hum of desire in his veins and James placed the empty glass back on the sideboard without the previous tremble in his fingers.

A full quarter hour later, the door opened and Rafe swung in, with his usual fierce expression. Gone was the open-eyed way he'd stared at James' hand as he'd pinned up his empty pants leg. If he hadn't known any better, he would've thought Rafe was as hot for him as he was. In reality, the expression was probably embarrassment at needing James' help.

"I think I would be too stubborn to ask for help. I'm sorry if I overstepped before."

Rafe raised one eyebrow. "It was just a pin. Thank you."

Just a pin—in other words, Rafe hadn't noticed the way James had almost salivated as he'd knelt at Rafe's feet.

"Shall we sit?"

"I take it from the fancy invitation that was left beside my bed yesterday that this is another of your reminiscing attempts."

James' cheeks prickled with heat. It was impossible not to be hurt by the snideness in Rafe's voice. "The point isn't for me to remember old times, but rather to give you a taste of…"

"What I missed by being a valiant soldier who damned near gave his life for his country? I may as well have." Rafe sneered. A lessor man would give up and buckle under his glare. James had always been attracted to strong leadership types, and the intense glare only made his chest swell and his skin tingle.

"I suppose you could take it that way... If you were so inclined to think the worst of me."

Rafe didn't answer and James clenched his teeth together so he didn't babble, or worse, admit his desire for Rafe. It should be bloody obvious by now.

"I don't think the worst of you, James. I'm just tired of being pitied, for only being seen as a returned soldier."

"That's not how I see you." James swallowed down the sudden thistle-like lump in his throat. "You are my friend, and I ..." He paused. "I suppose you are partially right. I do I feel guilty for not helping the war effort. For spending my time here, safely, eating good food, while others suffered through rationing or fighting or whatever. I've been incredibly lucky in that respect and I wanted to share that good fortune with my friend." He forced himself to stop there. It was the truth, albeit a partial truth, because he didn't say how he wanted shower Rafe with everything he had. To show him how much he adored him.

"I don't want your guilt, James. We all know why you didn't fight. No one blames you for a childhood illness. Damn it—" Rafe thumped one of his crutches on the floor. "Knowing you were safe, and at least one of my friends would survive this fucking war helped get me through."

James wanted to feed the hunger in Rafe's voice, to keep it safely inside him forever. "I... ahh, I'm glad to have been a source of..." He stopped, unable to continue as he realised what Rafe had said. One of my friends. James tried to ignore the way disappointment opened up like a pit in the floor that he wanted to jump into and disappear. Only a couple of days ago, he'd been concerned that the post-war Rafe wasn't same the person he'd always loved, but now as Rafe dismissed their friendship as being only one of many for him, James knew the depth of his unrequited love would forever bring him to his knees. He wasn't special to Rafe. He only wished he was.

"Damn it. Stop looking like I kicked your dog. The idea of the Christmas dinners is fine. Shall we eat?" Rafe sat in his chair and James forced himself to join him. Every step was difficult, a reminder of when he'd first recovered from polio and had to build the strength back in his body. The partial paralysis had never completely healed, but over time, he'd gained enough strength to compensate. His cane helped him balance, an integral part of him. Like the pining fool he was, he'd had the handle of this cane carved from a rock Rafe had given him before the war. It'd been a silly thing, the rock Rafe had tripped over while walking backwards through a paddock and talking about how lucky James was to have his job at the farm. Rafe's father, Lord Stanmore, still ran their family properties, and Rafe had gone on and on about how he wanted more responsibility but his father wanted him to go and get life experience. The irony in that moment was that Rafe went to war, in part to satisfy his father's requirements, although from the way James remembered Rafe's excitement at the time, Rafe had been keen to go and be a hero for his country.

"Is there a problem?"

James flicked out his napkin and laid it in his lap. He breathed in deep. "Why do you ask?"

"Your face paled."

"Damned Scottish complexion. How did I get that and

not the famed Tulloch blue eyes?" He had his mother's hazel eyes. Hers had flecks of green, while he'd lucked out completely and ended up with grey tints, more like the reflection of a cloud on a muddy pond.

Rafe shrugged. "You are the pedigree expert. One assumes you'd have a clue about inheritance."

The deep belly laugh that flew out of his mouth and rang too loud in the small dining room had nothing much to do with Rafe's jest and everything to do with the momentary piece of old-Rafe charm. And with that thought, the laughter dissipated. He had to stop comparing his friend with the past and just enjoy him as he was now. Gruff with little hints of charm, rather than charming without a care.

"Rafe! If you must know—"

"—I must, especially after that outburst."

"I must seem unhinged to you. And perhaps to myself as well. Since you went to war, I've had many conflicting emotions. And the laugh was merely overwrought as I miss your pithy sense of humour. To hear it here in my house is a gift greater than I could ever give in return." James knew how desperate he sounded for Rafe's attention, and yet, it was the truth.

"Conflicting emotions?"

James picked up his napkin and dabbed at the corner of his mouth, for no reason, except to give him time to compose his errant thoughts. "Obviously guilt because I couldn't go. Oh, I did my part, and bred many horses for the army, but it's a detached type of help."

"You didn't want to go, trust me." Rafe's voice deepened and it worsened the lump in James' stomach because it sent gooseflesh rising on his arms, as if Rafe had dragged a horse-hair brush over his skin, igniting all his nerve endings.

"Logic doesn't come into feelings, Rafe."

Rafe's mouth kicked up at the side. "Isn't that the truth? Look, I haven't been the best of friends either. I healed from this damned injury over a year ago, and I haven't visited until now."

James stilled. "Why?" He wasn't sure he wanted to know.

"Look at me, James. I'm not the same."

"And yet, you are the same. You made the pedigree joke, just like you would've before the war."

"But..."

James held up his hand. "No, wait. Of course, I've noticed a difference. You are harder, more fierce, less charming than you were, but none of that matters to me. You are still my best friend in all the world—" James cleared his throat and stared out the window as heat built behind his eyes.

"I am?"

"Of course you are. I didn't write a letter every month to anyone else. I'm not recreating Christmas dinners for anyone else."

Rafe scoffed quietly. "You might be."

"I'm not. I understand. The war changed us all, some more than others, but fundamentally, Rafe, you are still my friend, and I want to know you." James couldn't be clearer than if he'd lain naked on the floor in front of Rafe and begged him to suck his cock. He shivered as desire ran down his spine. What he really wanted was a kiss—a simple kiss with Rafe—the rest could grow from there.

"Trust me. You don't want to know what the war was

like. It can't be described. Not the constant noise, the mud, fucking trench foot... I lost seven horses, James. Seven. And countless colleagues." Rafe ignored James' plea to know about him, crucially ignoring the "you" in his sentence and sticking to the war only. "Damn it, look at me. I'll never be the same."

James stood up and walked the few steps around the table to Rafe. He wanted to hold his hand because he'd finally figured out the truth. He wasn't jealous of Rafe's athletic ability nor relieved that he'd lost that. He was deeply in love with a man who was hurting, a man who needed to be loved without any doubts.

"No, you trust me. These dinners aren't because I want you to be who you were before the war. Neither of us can be those people."

Rafe turned his head and their eyes met. "Then why?"

"Isn't it obvious?" James had done everything bar say the words. If he knelt down and held Rafe's hands, he couldn't be more overt than he was now.

"No. It's not obvious."

James' lips were suddenly dry and he licked them. "I'm attempting to woo you, Rafe. The horse, the letters, the intimate dinners..." His heart thudded so hard in his chest, he could barely hear himself talk.

"Oh." That was it. Rafe didn't want him. James turned to flee back to his seat, a laughable idea, that he could sit at the end of the table and have a formal dinner with Rafe after admitting such a thing. He'd only taken half a step, when Rafe grabbed his hand and pulled slightly. James turned, wishing he could wipe his clammy hands before Rafe held it.

"I didn't dare hope." Rafe's whisper was so quiet, James had to lean towards him. He wasn't sure he'd even heard correctly. His heart hammered so loud and somehow his breath roared loud in his ears as if he stood among the crowd cheering the winner over the last at Cheltenham.

CHAPTER FIVE

Rafe couldn't believe this moment could be happening. He'd dreamed of kissing James so many times, that it felt surreal to hear him state his actions in such overt terms. He'd been deliberately wooing Rafe? Rafe's next move had to matter. If he got this wrong, then the whole dinner was going to be awkward beyond his ability to imagine it.

"Shall we eat? I'm hungry." Rafe stalled, his mind empty as everything he'd ever wanted—James—stood awkwardly hopeful beside him. When James nodded stiffly and moved back to his own chair, Rafe's chest hollowed out. Wrong choice. James sat like a damned mannequin, rigid and unblinking, and it was Rafe's fault. If throwing his crutches through the window would help, he would do it. Of all the fucking ways to mess up, this had to be a greater screwup than standing on an unexploded grenade, only to have the blasted thing suddenly explode. The pain was the same, as if his whole body had once again crumpled, this time in slow motion. Naturally he'd made the wrong choice, because he was a wreck. He didn't mean physically. His body was a disappointment he was slowly becoming accustomed to. Inside his head, where no one could see, was the real wreck. Rafe might be good for a quick fucking, but he couldn't give James what he wanted. A relationship. Love.

"In 1915, it rained more than usual in the autumn. Our oat crop for the horses was smaller than expected, and it was impossible to buy it in from others as they all had the same problem." James prattled on in his lovely baritone, as if he really needed to fill the air with noise to cover up the lost intimacy of his declaration and Rafe's lack of response. It must be shock that made his torso tight into a knot because he'd never shied at this type of thing before.

"Besides, the price of food had started to sky-rocket because so much of it was imported and shipping was problematic..."

Rafe growled under his breath, glad for the distraction from James' declaration. Only someone who was protected from the war would describe the bombing of ships in such distant polite terms as problematic. The difference between them never seemed as big as it did right now. Whenever the war was mentioned, Rafe would be on edge like this—his brain only wanted to destroy things—it was why he couldn't be what James needed or deserved. Rafe was only good at one thing. Destruction.

"...and it was much more profitable to sell to people than to horses." James fiddled with his napkin again, a motion that made Rafe grind his teeth together.

"James."

"Yes?"

"I don't particularly care for a weather report." Rafe snapped at James and hated the way he flinched. Only moments ago, James had admitted to wooing Rafe. He should be kissing him, not arguing with him about inanities.

"Understood." James stood up and pulled the bell. "I suppose we should eat."

"Yes. I was already late to the table…" Rafe's mouth dried as he recalled the way James had knelt before him to pin up his pants leg. "What is on the menu for tonight?" He would find a way to apologise once the shock of their mutual attraction wore off enough that he could think. He'd spent his entire adult life lusting after James with the certainty that it wasn't reciprocated. To discover he'd misread the situation meant James had completed the job of turning him into a basket case. He growled again. He hated that damned term. It'd been used for soldiers so badly injured that they had to be carried off to the hospital in a basket. He'd been one, and for the first time he understood how it had expanded in meaning to describe someone who was an emotional wreck, not just a physical one. The surges of hot and cold through his body swirled in his veins in a river of confusion. Want. Lust. Agony. Pain. They were all so closely related.

"Lamb roast. Potatoes were hard to come by in 1915, thanks to the rain. We had a reasonable crop in our kitchen garden here, but we sold them all to those in need and went without for our own tables. Instead we had glazed carrots, roasted leeks with bacon, and roasted butternut squash. We also had a starter with pumpkin soup—the pumpkins loved the extra rain and we had an abundance of them—so it was pumpkin with everything for months."

"I don't feel sorry for you. I ate from a can for years." Anger might sustain him through the gut wrenching disappointment of his own reaction to James. If he'd fucked up and he couldn't have the one thing he wanted, he'd rather have nothing. Bully beef for the rest of his days.

James sighed, and the light flush on his cheeks grew darker. "That's not what I meant. I wish you would assume my motives are for the best, not an attempt to gloat over what we had and you didn't. I want to share lovely things with you."

Rafe ignored the twitch in his jaw. Presumably this was where he should apologise, but the words rested, all bitter on his tongue. "Wine?"

"Yes please. Stewart can serve it." The door opened in the most perfect timing, and Stewart set his trolley to the side and poured the wine into the crystal glasses. Once again, the table was decorated with Christmas themed... well, stuff. Flowers and all manner of pretty little bits and pieces. James had gone to a lot of effort to recreate this for him. Stewart had probably done the actual work, but even so, James had to go to the bother of organising it all. As the door closed with a thud and Stewart left them alone, understanding hit Rafe as if he'd fallen off his horse and all his breath pushed out of him by the impact. He had to apologise. He might not deserve James but that didn't mean James needed his anger flung at him for no apparent reason.

Rafe gulped down some wine. Dutch courage they called it. "Overby Christmas has nothing wrong with her. You gave me an expensive gift because..."

"Because you matter to me, Rafe."

"Brave, incredible James. You don't deserve someone like me. I had no idea you felt like that."

James shrank in his seat. "I kept it a secret, as much as I could. But look where it has gotten me. I've ruined our friendship with my declaration."

Rafe's heart almost burst from pressure. "No. Please no. You haven't ruined anything." If anyone had destroyed the potential between them it was him. "You surprised me, that's all."

"You don't hate me?"

"I could never hate you, James. I'm your friend. I always will be." And a bloody coward who couldn't tell James how he truly felt.

"Friend."

Rafe closed his eyes and sucked in a deep breath. "A friend who would like to kiss you." The strangled noise from the end of the table had Rafe instantly on his foot, his hands on the table for balance. "Are you well?"

"Yes. I would like you to kiss me." James' nostrils flared and his cheeks were bright pink. He couldn't look more perfectly kissable if he tried. Rafe grabbed his crutches and moved quickly towards James. They met halfway. Incredibly, James was just as keen as himself, except James stopped, a few inches before him. There was a moment in war, just before a charge, where everything felt like it paused and time stretched before complete chaos was unleashed with all the noise and drama and horror. Rafe could feel it now, that same pause, and he hesitated, unsure if he wanted the next moment. He wanted the next moment. He just didn't want to hurt James who wanted more than one moment.

"I'd forgotten that you are taller than me." Rafe forced a laugh and it burned like mustard gas on his throat. Everyone forgot how tall James was, and it did Rafe no credit at all to be just like everyone else. He was built like a boxer; medium height and broad.

"Three inches." The same distance as they stood apart. Near. Close enough for James' breath to be warm on Rafe's skin. It blew on him and send waves skittering over his face and throat. His fingers held onto his crutches tight. If James moved one inch closer, he'd practically taste his Burgundy-scented breath. Doubt circled, like a hawk over a corpse.

"I'm sorry. I can't do this. Can we eat?" Rafe retreated, rushing back to his chair.

"Can't or won't?"

Rafe's crutches clattered on the floor as he sat down awkwardly too fast. "I don't know James. I've spent years absolutely certain that you couldn't possibly want me like that. That you would find a nice wife and make yourself a happy family. I need time to adjust to this news."

"Fine." The hurt in James' voice vibrated in Rafe's chest, as if he were collecting all of James' aches in his own heart. The war had stripped him of his charm. He could never be someone's long term person.

"Please. Just give me time." It was the closest to an apology that Rafe could manage. He'd faced down whole armies with less fear than the cold chill circulating in his veins right now.

After a long silence, James cleared his throat. "Shall I serve dinner?"

"Thank you." Rafe waited awkwardly. "You didn't answer my question about a wife."

James placed a plate full of food before Rafe, then returned to his seat. His usual relaxed way of moving seemed more... deliberate than usual. "That was a question?"

"Wasn't it? You don't want a wife?"

The sigh James let out was so loud it practically knocked over the candle holder. "What part of I've been wooing you for over six years gave you the impression I might want a wife?"

Rafe gulped. He'd really made a mess of this, and why? He wanted to kiss James more than almost anything. Damn it, he'd lusted over James' arse just before dinner. Had jerked off imagining it was James' hands on his cock, not his own.

"I wouldn't rule it out. My own grandfather had a much hushed up affair with a man before he married, and if I had to hazard a guess about Lord St. George—"

James raised one eyebrow. "Yes, I know about my own father's exploits as a spy. He took me aside as a young man and let me know he understood. One of the reasons he'd been so successful was because he'd found it easy to get pillow secrets from the men and women of influence. He could go directly to the source, as well as the gossip and second-hand reports from wives and mistresses."

"Your father admitted that?"

"To me. Not the world, although I imagine his handlers knew. They'd probably selected him for the job knowing he had more skills than his ability with languages." James sighed. "It doesn't matter, but he did tell me life would be easier if I had no preference and could decide to choose a wife, but he would not judge me if that wasn't possible for me."

A lightness covered Rafe, as if he'd finally dropped his military kit with gun and pack, and he shook his head. "You were right the other day. We are so lucky."

"Life might be easier if I wasn't purely a molly, but here we are. No wife for me." James crossed his arms and leaned back in his chair, as if daring Rafe to disagree.

"Same. I only discussed this once with my parents."

"You mentioned it?"

Rafe scoffed. "No, I'm not brave enough. Before the war, there was a rumour and Father took me aside and asked me. That's when I heard about grandfather's affair. Mother was a bit shocked at the time. After the war she told me she realised how sheltered she'd been before the war, and it was fine with her as long as I was happy." The idea that his mother considered herself naïve was amusing—she'd literally married his father as an alibi to stop him being accused of murdering her fiancé. She'd slept with at least two men before marriage, yes one of them was his father, and yet she found the concept of him lusting after a man challenging. He couldn't fault her, she'd always loved him, and she'd taken the time to learn and accept. She might have been a pain in the arse when he was healing—damned doctor wanting him to focus on getting better when all he wanted to do was be miserable—but that also came from a place of motherly love.

"I can't imagine how good that would feel to be accepted when you hadn't been before. I wasn't nervous because I'd guessed from Father's stories about his glory days. You know, before he met Mother and gave up spying to be with her on the farm here." James unfolded his arms. "I want you to be happy, Rafe."

His name on James' breath sent a shiver up his spine. "So do I. More than anything. But I don't know if I can anymore."

"Take your time. Eat the roast lamb and save me a kiss for later."

Rafe shivered. "A nightcap?"

James licked his lips. "Yes," he croaked. Rafe had many regrets in his life but none topped this one. It would be so easy to kiss James, to trace his tongue down his throat, lower and lower until he licked the end of James' cock. He wanted to cup his balls, lightly stroke between his legs, and then suck him until he screamed with joy. Rafe stabbed a carrot with his fork and ate it. The sweetness of the glazing reminded him that James was too succulent to toy with. Rafe might be able to make James scream and come, but he couldn't be there for him for the rest of his days. He almost choked on the bloody carrot as his throat thickened. The more food he ate, with James so close, the more it turned to ash on his tongue until he may as well be inhaling the dregs from the fireplace.

CHAPTER SIX

After a terrible night's sleep, James parked the car beside the stable block. His good sprinter, Sunshine Joy, had been soundly beaten by Diadem in the July Cup ten days ago, and had arrived home from the trainer's stables to spell. He stepped out of the car, ignoring Rafe, and walked through the archway towards the main office. Rafe had insisted on coming with him to inspect the horse, then hadn't spoken at all on the half-mile car ride from the main house to the stables. James didn't know why he bothered, and to be honest, he was still confused about their discussion last night. Did Rafe want him or not?

James tried to ignore the burr of irritation, like a stone in his shoe. He needed to focus on work. They'd lost a lot of staff to the Spanish flu and between that and the war it was difficult to employ new people to take their spaces. Poor old Frank was doing the work of three men, although lucky the foaling season had ended a couple of months ago, and the current workload was less than in spring. During the spring,

James had mucked out boxes and helped sweep up after the end of the day. He wished he could do more; having to use his cane for balance meant he couldn't carry feed or water buckets.

"Frank. How is she?"

Frank walked quickly towards him with a big grin on his wrinkled old face. "She was galloped on during the Cup and one of those cuts is going to take a while to heal." The old jockey had fallen too many times in his career and now his body was stiff where all the old injuries had healed, although he still walked at a decent clip. He was an excellent judge of a horse and James trusted his opinion. When Frank had caught the Spanish flu last autumn, James had nursed him back to health in the main house. Of course, Frank's cottage was clean and warm, but he lived alone there now, having been widowed a few years before. Stewart hadn't been happy about bringing the illness into the main house—well, those days were gone now, and Frank was still with them. Thank God.

"Foster said as much. He thinks she'll be fine for a short autumn campaign."

Frank scratched his head. "I'm not sure. Perhaps you should retire her. She'll make a fine broodmare."

"You don't agree with Foster?" James had worked out the timing and even with a month off now, Sunshine Joy would be ready for a race in late November. She could have a short campaign before a longer spell, then be back for another crack at the July Cup next year.

"I think she'll be fit enough again by late autumn, but she's never been much good on a wet track, so why push her?"

"Good point." James could send her to a stallion in early January and she'd have a nice early foal the following season. If he chased the July Cup again with her, it'd be another year before she went to stud, and she probably wasn't in the same class as this year's winner Diadem. "Yes, let's retire her."

"Oh, hello. I didn't realise you had a friend visiting, sir." Frank stared past James and he turned to see Rafe leaning sardonically on his crutches.

"This is Rafe, you must remember him. He virtually grew up here."

Frank, who could tell twelve almost identical bay fillies apart, squinted in Rafe's direction. "I'm afraid I don't recall you."

"Lord Stanmore's oldest son. He took Charles of Arrott as his war mount," James said.

"Good horse, that Charles of Arrott. What happened to him?" Frank asked.

"Shot. Just as I should've been. If I was a horse, they would've put me down, but sadly humans are required to suffer."

"Rafe!"

Rafe shrugged. "It's true. Horses get the benefit of quality of life, while I'm left to cope with quantity of life. No one asked me if I wanted this."

James almost reached out for him, almost said that he wanted Rafe, but only nodded.

"You and me both. This old body of mine has had more broken bones than any human ought to have suffered through, but I'm glad I'm still here. You'll figure how to deal with it; just as old Spymaster has learned to cope with his terrible suspensory injury."

James could've hugged Frank. "Spymaster is Frank's hack."

"Was. The old bugger has been retired for a decade now. He slipped badly one winter while herding sheep and did a suspensory. Spent months on box rest and walks like our James now. But he's comfortable and he likes watching over the yard. So you see, we don't put down our horses if they have a chance at a decent life, and you'll discover the same."

Rafe didn't respond. If it wasn't for the deep frown, James might have wondered if he'd heard Frank's version of a motivating speech at all.

"I take it you put Sunshine Joy in the box beside Spymaster?"

"Yes. She's a typical mare, grumpy at being boxed, and she's already taken a nip out of one of the lads today."

"Spymaster will help her settle."

Frank nodded. "I believe so. He's the best companion for the surly ones." If only James could convince Rafe that he could also be a good companion for Rafe's grumps.

"I'll get her out of the box and you can take a look for yourself." Frank walked away, leaving James and Rafe alone, well, as alone as possible could be in a stable block.

"I'm sorry. I should have dealt with that introduction a little better. I forget that it can be shock for people who remember you."

Rafe raised one eyebrow. "What else could you have done aside from pretend I'm someone I'm not? I mean, he said the horse walks like you, and we know what that means." Judging

by the sneer in Rafe's tone, he obviously thought poorly of
Frank's attempt to cheer him up.

"Old Frank doesn't mean anything by that. He thinks in
horse, and unsound is only a descriptor of action, not a reflection on one's character."

"You are more forgiving than me."

James shrugged one shoulder. "Or perhaps I simply have
known him for a long time and understand what he means."
A humph sound was Rafe's only response. James wanted to
continue; that neither of them should have to learn to put
up with the way people talked about them, but he'd had his
paralysis since he was five years old. He'd become resigned to
other people's nonsense. It quickly sorted out good people
from the shallow ones, and he was able to eliminate the
nasty ones from his life with rapidity. But before he could
reassure Rafe that it wasn't all terrible, Frank came back
leading Sunshine Joy, whose flattened ears effectively
demonstrated that her personality was nothing like her
name.

"You have a gift, James." Rafe's voice changed, with an
unexpected note of humour, and it took all of James' concen-
tration not to spin around and gape at him.

"Oh?"

"Overby Christmas, Sunshine Joy. Please don't name a
horse Sound and Fast, the damned thing would break down
before you could saddle it."

Frank laughed quietly under his breath. "Everyone in
racing knows better than to jinx a horse with a name that
implies soundness. Even using a speed reference is asking for
trouble."

"And I don't think you could blame my naming of Overby Christmas for the length of the war."

Rafe grinned. "Perhaps Sunshine Joy is an aspirational name too? Was she this grumpy as a yearling?"

"Her dam is a nasty one too, so yes, there is an element of that in her name."

"A horse doesn't know their name." Frank handed the lead rope to James and ran his hand along the horse's back, down her hind leg, and started to undo the bandage. "This one is the worst. The other leg is merely superficial." Once the bandage was off, they swapped places again, and James shifted so he could inspect the injury.

"She was bloody lucky they didn't both fall. That's nasty." The other horse's front hoof had stripped the skin off the back tendon on Sunshine Joy's hind leg. "Damned lucky. No wonder she pulled up at the last furlong."

"Yes, being galloped on is not her fault, and I think the jockey did a good job. She would've felt terrible in her action almost immediately. He probably saved her from a nastier injury by easing her out of the race so quickly."

"If we can keep any infection out, she'll heal well." The wound had already started to heal and if they could stop it from going proud, then it might not even scar.

"Foster..." Frank turned his face towards Rafe, "That's the trainer. He's right. She'll heal well enough to go back into work. But she's a five year-old now, and she's already proven herself."

"Yes. Let's get her well, and then we can retire her sound. She'll be easier to manage as a broodmare if she has no issues going forward." James would have liked to have had a top class race on her resume, however, Frank was right especially if this year's winner Diadem returned to defend her title in the race. It would be almost a year before the tracks firmed to Sunshine Joy's liking again. If she'd been comfortable on softer surfaces, he might have given her one more campaign. Frank led the mare over to a tie-up stall where she could stand in the cross-ties while he cleaned the wound and rebandaged it.

"I thought I'd ride out and check some of the young stock. Would you like to come along?"

Rafe's expression darkened. "James. I can't ride."

"Why not? I can manage." James was left standing with his mouth hanging open as Rafe whirled around on his crutches and disappeared. What had he said wrong? Rafe had always been a brilliant rider. The small fact of a missing leg wouldn't change that. He could do what James did, use a dressage crop for the leg aids on his weaker side, similar to the way ladies did when they rode in a side saddle.

Fury and disappointment had charged Rafe's body as he'd bolted from the stables. Of all the things for James to say, how dare he expect Rafe to ride a horse? Of course, storming back from the stables to the main house had exhausted him. It was only half a mile, but the result of his outburst was an afternoon spent in bed in an uncomfortable sleep. The sunset shone with an eerie orange glow through his bedroom window when he woke hours later. His stomach rumbled. Fucking hell, he'd missed lunch and was late for dinner too.

The sun didn't set until quite late in the summer here. And his legs ached like the blazes. Even the missing one. His mother, ever the doctor, had mentioned that sometimes he might feel pain or itchiness in the missing leg. Phantom pains, doctors called them, but there was no treatment because it was all in his mind, or as Mother said, in his confused nerves. They'd been the worst in the months after the explosion and hadn't been this bad for months. It served him right. Rushing away in fury was an overreaction to James' request. Any rational person might have explained why going for a hack around the farm wasn't possible for him.

He pulled himself into a seated position and leaned forward to massage the leg that was still attached to him. The theory was that long slow motions with a clenched fist along the muscles would ease the tension until the soreness from overuse began to dissipate. The first stroke had him screaming in agony.

The door flew open. James.

"What on earth is wrong? You missed dinner."

Rafe glared at him. "I don't need a saviour." Had James been standing outside his door waiting for him to make a noise? Or was it an irritating coincidence that he'd been walking past right at the moment Rafe tried to help himself. If James had dropped by to tell him he'd missed dinner, he could've worked that out for himself by looking out the window at the bloody sunset, or by listening to his stomach grumble.

"I didn't offer that." James stood tall, his chin lifted high. "It was just a simple horse ride."

"Nothing about this is simple. How am I to get on the

horse? How do I stay on the horse? How do I steer the horse?" His sister had joked about riding side saddle and the idea had some merits, but he really didn't want to try and fail. Horse riding had been his favourite thing before the war. During it too. He'd rather never try than know with absolute certainty that he could never do it again. The real art of riding well was in using leg aids to guide the horse, a real rider could ride without saddle or bridle, not needing them if they had legs. It was fucking obvious.

"We can find a way. Frank has a friend who lost the bottom half of his leg in a racing fall, and he still rides. He uses a dressage whip in place of leg aids. Similar to side saddle."

"Half a leg isn't a whole leg." Why was he even debating this? It didn't distract him from his pain, only made everything tighter, more tense, more... brittle, until his breath burned his throat.

"Fine. Have it your way."

Rafe growled. "Yes. I don't want to sit on a plodding hack and walk around. I can go faster on my crutches." Just as he had this morning. Now he had to pretend he wasn't in pain from his own rash choice. "I'm never going to gallop across country and fly over fences again, so why bother?"

"Then you aren't going to try at all?"

Pain shot up his leg and stabbed him in the lower back. He attempted pithy response came out as a grunt.

"Are you certain you are fine? You look terrible." James frowned. "And you are clutching your knee."

"Am not." Rafe forced himself to stop pressing into the cramped muscles just above his knee but failed. This was why he couldn't kiss James because no one deserved to go through this with him. James would soon stop loving him when faced with the reality of Rafe's temper. He could barely spit out those two words without railing at James. Rafe ground his teeth so hard he knew his jaw would hurt later, but it was barely noticeable over the rest of it. If this pain got any worse, he'd rip the blasted leg off with his bare hands.

James sighed and sat on the bed beside Rafe's leg. "Stop being stubborn." He gently lifted Rafe's hands off his knee and started to slowly massage the joint. Rafe grunted again, then bit back a scream as the heel of James' hand stroked past the worst part of the cramp.

"Stop."

James stopped. After a few tense breaths, Rafe realised he may as well accept James' offer, otherwise he'd be here for hours in agony.

"Fine. Don't stop, but..." He dragged in a deep breath, struggling for air. "... please be gentle."

James nodded, then slowly stood up. "Wait here and take off your pants." James sped out of the room, his cane thumping louder than usual, while Rafe was still catching his breath. He wanted him to do what? Rafe rolled his head on his shoulders, his neck cracking satisfactorily, and tried to slow his racing pulse. He'd wanted distraction, hadn't he? He certainly had it now.

CHAPTER SEVEN

James could not believe he'd offered to massage Rafe's leg. He wanted to help his friend; naturally his first response was to help, or at least that was the excuse he could tell himself. Rafe was obviously in pain, with his usual frown even deeper, and a faint clammy sweat shone on his temples. What James couldn't believe and what really made his heart beat faster than a galloping horse was that in a moment of absurd bravery, he'd told Rafe to take off his pants. It was logical. He could massage oil into the skin and that would help ease the muscle cramps. He just didn't expect to be touching Rafe in such an intimate, and yet a distant, way. Cook had a special skin oil she made from lanolin, beeswax, and petroleum jelly, with a rosehip scent, that he used on his own limbs when they got sore from overuse. It'd be perfect for Rafe. The only difficult part now was that James had to fulfil his offer without completely losing control of himself. He'd be touching Rafe. Blast and oh fuck, so amazing, all at the same time.

He grabbed the jar of Cook's handmade skin oil from his bedroom, tucked it in his jacket pocket, and made his way back to Rafe's room. He leaned his cane against the wall, opened the door, then used his shoulder to keep the door open as he grabbed his cane again. The manoeuvre meant he didn't see Rafe's naked leg until he was inside the room.

"Oh."

Rafe sighed. "Come on now. Surely you've seen wounds before."

"Yes. I just expected—" James swallowed as a lump in his throat formed. He'd expected to see a nasty scar where Rafe's leg had been amputated. When he'd first heard about the accident, his first instinct was to ask his mother what the verdict would be. She'd described cauterising the wound to prevent infection—a process that sounded horrific—and now he could see the result, his chest almost caved in on itself with hurt for Rafe. What surprised him was the red mess of scars on his other leg.

"Having one's leg exploded off doesn't happen cleanly. I was lucky to keep one leg." The calm, almost clinical tone of Rafe's voice told James how tightly he was holding in his annoyance. James nodded. He aimed for the same level of calm and hoped Rafe wouldn't notice the quiver in his voice.

"That makes sense. Well, I have this jar of oil. I guess you'd call it massage oil. Are you allergic to sheep? Anyway, Cook makes it for me. It's lanolin and petroleum jelly and some other stuff." Now he was babbling like a nervous school boy. Damn it. James breathed in and made his way over to the bed. How was he going to manage this? "Ahh, perhaps if you shuffle to the edge of the bed, I can pull up a chair and sit beside you and that will give me the best, ahhh—"

"Leverage?"

James cleared his throat. "Yes." He put the jar on the bed and proceeded to grab a little wooden chair from beside a small writing desk at the corner of Rafe's room and shift it over to the bed. His hands were a little clammy, damned nerves. When he placed the chair and sat down, Rafe's leg was right there in front of him. Exactly what he'd asked for. He reached for the jar. His fingers slipped on the lid, and he had to wipe them on his pants before a second attempt. Phew. He breathed in deep and dipped his fingers into the jar. The cool solid oil started to melt under the warmth of his hands, and he spread it over Rafe's skin. James had expected a spark or a shock when he touched Rafe because that's what usually happened when he became careless and accidentally touched him. It didn't come. James kept his gaze directly on Rafe's knee as he massaged the oil into his skin. Softly at first, long strokes to learn the shape of his muscles. When James was younger, Frank had taught him how to massage a horse to help them recover from exercise. It took long strokes down each muscle, gently feeling where any tightness was, and slowly easing across the taut sections to stretch them out. This was the same technique. Over and over, James placed his hands on the middle of Rafe's thigh, then stroked down the muscles towards the knee, around each side of the kneecap, and finishing just after the joint. Each time, he pressed slightly harder, listening carefully for Rafe's breathing. When Rafe winced and emitted a little growl, James stopped.

"Too hard?"

"A little but it's good. It's ... helping."

James nodded, again without looking at Rafe's face. It helped detach him if he focused on the leg and relieving the sore muscles. Touching Rafe was less intimate if he didn't think about it being Rafe. Concentrate on the job at hand and don't connect it to the one person he'd been in love with forever, otherwise the flutter in his stomach would turn into a storm.

"Roll over."

"Excuse me?"

James swallowed. "Please roll over. I'll do your calf muscle now."

"Sure." Rafe shuffled on the bed, while James dug his fingers into the jar of oil. The petroleum jelly made the concoction set into almost a paste that melted with a little bit of heat, like the warmth of his own skin. He didn't wanted to think about the warmth of Rafe's skin. The back of Rafe's knee wasn't as scarred as the front, although it could just be the angle. Most of the damage was on the inside of his knee, which was now pointing away from James. He spread the oil over Rafe's thigh, down his hamstring, over the knee, and down over the calf muscle. It took another swipe from the jar to cover Rafe's Achilles tendon, heel, and the arch of his foot. James cradled Rafe's heel with his hands and used his thumbs to massage the arch of Rafe's foot. He flinched a little.

"Sore?"

"Tickles."

James pressed harder to try and ease the ticklish sensation. Rafe cried out.

'Sorry."

"It's good. Don't be sorry. I didn't even know that part of me was tight."

James spent plenty of time on Rafe's foot, switching between soothing strokes and deep muscle work, until his thumbs were a little sore from his efforts. He shifted in his chair and began to work on Rafe's calf muscle. First with long slow strokes up the thick muscle. Gentle, gentle. Then firmer as Rafe's breathing slowed down. With the heels of his hands, James could get good pressure behind each stroke and soon he could feel the muscle fibres begin to relax and straighten out. The work became rhythmic. When James lengthened his stroke to include the bottom of the hamstring, Rafe cried out in pain, and James jerked his hands off his task.

"Sorry."

"Don't. Be. Sorry." Rafe bit out each word. James nodded, and gently laid his hands over the base of Rafe's hamstring where the thick muscle attached to the joint. No wonder Rafe had reacted, the end of the muscle was a tight ball, a large knot of fibres. It must hurt like the blazes. He placed one hand on Rafe's calf, just below the knee, and with the other began to work on the knot. Each stroke ended with a stretch between his two hands. Once again, James listened carefully to the way Rafe's breath hitched, or settled, as he worked on the muscle to ease it out.

"I think that's enough." Rafe finally spoke and James blinked as he glanced at his watch. Oh, he'd been doing this for nearly an hour. He reached into his pocket and wiped his hands on a handkerchief.

"Absolutely. I hope that helps."

"Yes. It feels much better." Rafe cleared his throat and

rolled over. "James?"

He hummed, and kept his gaze firmly on the bed, away from Rafe.

"Please look at me."

James breathed out slowly, then flung his head around, almost giving himself a sore neck in his effort to avoid looking at Rafe's body. Rafe's underwear clad cock, more like. His throat thickened and dried out.

"Thank you very much."

James nodded, not wanting to automatically say "My pleasure" and all that that implied. He stood up, his knees slightly weak, and grabbed his cane. The carved rock, Rafe's rock, on top of his cane slipped in his hands. Damned massage oil. He fumbled for the handkerchief again, nearly whacking Rafe's knee as he tried to sort out the new tremble in his hands. His heart could have drummed the entirety of Sophie Tucker's song Some of these Days before he managed to collect himself enough to leave the room.

"I'll see you at dinner tomorrow then." Rafe called out.

"Um, yes. Dinner. 1916." James bolted before he rushed back and kissed Rafe hard on the mouth. The problem was that he'd already offered that and Rafe had rejected him. He wasn't sure his heart could cope with being rejected again. No, that was too harsh. Rafe had told him to wait, to give him time to adjust to James' declaration. James wished he understood what it was that made Rafe want to wait. He was almost desperate enough to offer to change himself for Rafe. Down that path lay misery; more pain than the initial rejection, so he would stay strong, stay himself, and simply wait with hope. It burrowed into his chest, lodged there.

CHAPTER EIGHT

A whole day went past without Rafe seeing James and he missed him. It was his own goddamned fault, though. Dear James, always trying to help. Whether he wanted it or not. Rafe supposed he'd better drag his carcass to dinner, given it was yet another one of James' *'cheer up Rafe by giving him a ton of Christmases'* dinner. 1916 hadn't been a great year for him. He'd had his leg blasted off only a few months before at the front near Varennes and had spent fuck knows how long in various hospitals. He punched the pillow on his bed. He didn't precisely know how long he'd been in hospital because the date when his whole world changed was unknown. It'd been autumn, sometime in October or maybe early November. Presumably one of the officers knew the date; it'd be written in his records if he ever decided he needed to know to gory details. He'd deliberately chosen to be a cavalry soldier, not an officer, even though he could have used his birthright to walk into the senior job with no experience. The entire point of him going to war was to gain the necessary experience, so it seemed ridiculous the army would put him in charge of men without having earned it just because of the good fortune of his birth.

Rafe folded up the pants leg and pinned it before he pulled them on. He wasn't going to go through the humiliation of needing James to sort that out for him again. James already did too much. For a second he wondered if he should turn up to the re-enactment dinner wearing the cotton gown he'd ended up wearing in hospital. The army took his uniform—what was left of it—and recycled it for another poor soul. No, a decent shirt, and a vest to cover his suspenders. It was too hot for a jacket tonight.

"Good evening." The door to the dining room was already open, which he appreciated as he didn't have to fuss about with his crutches.

James blushed a little. "Good evening, Rafe. I'm so glad you feel well enough to attend tonight."

"Thank you. It was your massage that really did the trick." He rather enjoyed the way James' features became pinker, even on his throat, although sadly he wore a tie so Rafe couldn't see the soft hollow at the base of his throat. What a shame. That was one of Rafe's favourites places to kiss on a man, where the stubble ended and before any chest hair began, a little secret place where he could be nuzzle against and feel someone's pulse against his mouth.

"I wasn't sure about tonight. 1916 wasn't the best year for you, and I didn't want to bring back any bad memories, but I spent some time going back through old newssheets and they said that the hospitals had tried their best to bring Christmas cheer to all the patients."

"James. It's fine. It might not have been a good year for me; a year of great change, one might say, but Father sent me a letter to say you had had an excellent year. A Guineas winner."

"Country Ravine, yes. She has a lovely colt at foot this year. Of course, 1917 was better for you as Sunny Jane won the Oaks."

Rafe sat down before the slight wobble in his knee turned worse. The leg was still ginger after his mad half-mile dash across country. "Why was that better for me?"

"Sunny Jane is out of a half-sister to Overby Christmas, and is by Sunstar, the sire of your colt."

"Our colt." Rafe persisted in being accurate over his ownership.

"Yes. Our colt. Would you like some wine to start?"

Rafe nodded. "Yes please. What is on the menu tonight?"

"I wanted to do a proper York Ham, but of course, they take two months to cure, and it's summer now, so the demand for them isn't as high as at Christmas."

Rafe tried not to be disappointed. "I do love a good ham."

James smiled. "I know. That's why I telephoned the best supplier in the country to confirm they had one, then sent Stewart for a drive yesterday to York... it's a distance of 170 miles, so it took him all day... Cook has spent all day today preparing you a proper York Ham from Scotts of York."

"You sly devil. You had me believing I would get an inferior substitute."

James chuckled. "Only the best for you. We do cure our own hams here at Beaumount Stud, but of course, we have

Berkshire pigs and Gloucestershire Old Spots, not the Large White they use for the York Ham."

"I'm sure that makes a difference."

"It must, otherwise people wouldn't be line up to get their York Ham for Christmas every year."

Rafe leaned back in his chair. "Or send their staff for a whole day drive to go and buy one. I hope it lives up to the effort."

"Shall we see?" James pulled the bell, then made his way back to the table and poured a glass of wine for Rafe.

"This is about as far removed from my actual Christmas of 1916 as could be imagined, unless I was naked on a beach in the Pacific."

James' tongue darted out to moisten his lower lip and Rafe's muscles tightened, ready for action. If only he could get past his need to care for James, and just kiss him without worrying about the future.

"I don't particularly need to think about you naked. It's rather an unfair comment given you know how much I want you." James' rough voice sent prickles across Rafe's skin.

"I apologise."

"As you should. For so many years, I've loved you knowing it was hopeless, listening for any rumour that might … give me a chance and finding nothing, and now you have the …" James' chest rose and fell. "… audacity to tease me like this."

Oh, Rafe wanted to tease him in an entirely different fashion. "Yes, I see how my reticence might be causing you some frustration."

James thumped his fist on the table. "Only because I care.

Rafe. I have waited this long. You say you want to kiss me, but you want to wait. I can keep waiting for you."

A desperate lust filled Rafe's body with heat. The type of brilliant heat that was like sitting beside a fire on a cold winter day cuddled up naked under a blanket with another man. With limbs twisted together, and skin touching everywhere. Not that he'd ever done that, but he'd imagined it often enough as the combination of several individual moments. His blood ran hot. He could spend whole days intertwined with James beside the glow of a fire while outside snow fell. Cosy in the lull after sex. He opened his mouth to say yes when Stewart entered the room with his trolley from the kitchen.

"Celery gratin with crusty bread." Stewart handed Rafe a plate and took off the silver cover to reveal a cheesy little pie dish and two slices of toasted bread with herbed butter on the side. The scent of melted cheese filled his nostrils.

"Thank you, Stewart. Shall we have the main in about twenty minutes?" James nodded once.

"Of course, sir. Enjoy. Although why you want poverty food, I don't know."

James smiled. "We discussed this. I wanted the menu to reflect the rations we had to deal with in 1916. No oysters or eggs, and only the bacon and ham we could make here at Beaumount."

"Good for you, sir." Stewart obviously thought James had cracked it.

"I assure you it's a lot better than hospital slop, which is all that was available in Le Havre in 1916."

"My apologies."

Rafe waved his hand. "Don't be sorry. It's all part of life as a soldier."

"I'm not apologising for not understanding. I served as well, although my war service was short."

"Oh?"

Stewart rolled up his sleeve to reveal the edges of a nasty burn scar. "I was stretchered off in early 1915 after being burned. I was fortunate that it was early in the war and I was sent to Gillies burns unit at Sidcup to recover. The scarring is nasty, although I see that you have some experience with that." Now that Stewart mentioned it, Rafe could see the red scarring that wound up the side of his neck and into his hair line. "So you see, it is no hardship for me to spend the day driving to get the very best ham from Scotts of York for a fellow soldier."

"Thank you. I can see why you express some disbelief at James' choice of starter."

James cleared his throat, as if to remind them of his presence as they talked about him. "Celery gratin is delicious. The milk comes from a diary nearby and the celery is grown here in the kitchen garden."

"Yes, sir." Stewart bowed and with a little grin aimed at Rafe, he left the room.

"It says a lot about you, James."

James' eyes widened. "What does?"

"That your staff are so open with their opinions around you."

"Stewart has lived his entire life at Beaumount Stud. We held a job for him when he enlisted and said he could have the pick of positions when he returned, as we did with our other staff." James' expression shut down, and Rafe didn't have to ask to know he was thinking of those who hadn't returned.

"Shall we try this before it gets cold?" Rafe dug into the pie with his fork.

"I take it you slept well. You are chirper than usual." James said. Rafe held his fork in mid-air, hovering, unable to decide how, or if, he should respond. Before he could, James winked.

"It must be my massage."

Rafe almost dropped his fork. "James. You aren't helping here."

"Oh?"

"Damn it. Stop pouting."

James smirked. "I'm not pouting."

"Do you know why I won't kiss you, even though you tempt me?" Rafe growled on a short breath, unwilling to give James time to answer. "Because I can't be the chirpy—" Rafe paused purposefully since James had used that word already. "—person I was before the war. I can't be the man you think you love."

James glanced down at his plate. "I'm willing to take that chance."

"And if it doesn't pay off? This isn't one of your gambles. You aren't setting me for a race to get better odds on the day, James." Rafe spat out James' name.

"No. I don't care about the odds, not for this. I do care very much about you."

Rafe almost threw his napkin on the floor. "You don't understand."

"Then make me understand. I want to know."

"You really don't. You look at me and think the fucking missing leg is the worst of it. It's not. Even before that day, the war had changed me. I'm not the happy-go-lucky fellow who used to tease you. I can't be that."

James obviously had no common sense as he stared defiantly back at Rafe. "I'm not the same person I was six years ago either, Rafe." The way he threw Rafe's name back at him paralleled how Rafe wanted to use James' name as a weapon. He had to change his attack.

"Do you cry when a friend dies? What about a horse? Do you cry over your horses?"

"Yes. Doesn't everyone?"

Rafe sneered. "No. Not anymore. I lost seven horses during my short time at the war. I didn't even bother to name them after the third one died." Rafe could hardly breathe, his lungs begging for air with shallow pants. "I've lost count of the friends and colleagues I lost. If I cried for each of them, I'd spend my life in tears."

James blinked and Rafe held his breath anticipating a consoling comment. A commiseration. But nothing came. James simply waited.

"I don't know how many days I begged someone to put a bullet in me. I'd rather be dead than suffer; just put me down like I'd shot my injured and dying horses."

"I struggle to shoot my own horses, even when they are in pain and obviously won't recover. Nell was always going to become a veterinarian, I could tell when she had the instinct to know which ones would recover and which ones needed a quick end to stop their suffering."

Rafe laughed bitterly as James outlined why any kisses

between them could never happen. James had a good heart. He cared too much, and Rafe would only end up hurting him.

"I saw Nell early in the war. We stayed a night at her veterinary hospital. It was just after Charlie was shot, and I ended up collecting a new horse from her boss. Joe. He was a good sort, a typical crossbreed with good bone. He lasted seven months before he broke his neck in a fall." Rafe ground his teeth together. It would be so easy to let James' expression soften him, but no, he needed to be harsh to destroy the bond that pulled him towards James.

"Poor Joe."

Rafe growled. "Triumph was next, but he got the colic from bad hay, and then I stopped naming them."

"Colic. What an ordinary way to go." James pressed his fingers to the bridge of his nose.

"Nothing was ordinary in the war. He would never have had colic if he'd been fed properly. There was no grass, only dusty hay and a rancid bran mash. Better than nothing, until..." Rafe couldn't continue. From the moment James had accused him of being chirpy, he'd deliberately tried not to be so charming, but the weight of years of hurt didn't sustain him. Not with James patiently listening. He wanted Stewart to arrive back in the room with the bloody ham—anything to break up this knot inside him. Instead, he dipped his fork into the gratin and began to eat. The rich cheese filled pie melted on his tongue, a reminder that he wasn't at war anymore. He'd come home and was able to eat incredible food with flavours like this. Life wasn't all the misery that his brain kept reminding him about. Maybe over time, his nightmares would fade like they did every dawn as the daylight brought a new day. It was a miracle how a simple celery and cheese pie could warm him on the inside and bring a snippet of hope.

"James?"

"Yes."

"I'm sorry about Charlie. He was a good horse." Rafe was really apologising about himself, his attitude, and his inability to give James what he clearly wanted. Love, companionship, incredible sex... He could definitely do the latter, but would it be worth it without the first two elements?

"You don't need to apologise for doing your job, Rafe."

"If you knew what it was like, then you'd know you are wrong."

James shrugged. "I'm sure you'll tell me when you are ready."

"What if I'm never ready?" Rafe knew it was impossible. He couldn't even imagine what that would be like.

"I'm not asking for the whole saga in one giant story. I can wait for little pieces when they are relevant. You aren't a history book that I need to read in a week, Rafe. You're a person with all the complexities that come with that." James rolled his eyes. "Besides, we read history at Eton, and it was bloody boring."

Rafe laughed despite himself. "It was. And I'm sure there will be endless books written on this war. Every aspect analysed forever because it's the Great War. The war to end all wars."

"Careful, your bitterness is showing." James winked and Rafe felt his grin stretch his cheeks. The sensation was unusual—it'd been too long since he'd really smiled properly.

"Thank you, James. Really and truly thank you. It's so easy to get trapped into, as you say, bitterness. Many things in the war weren't fair... well, that's the—"

"—nature of war?" James interrupted.

"Yes. And now I have to live my life knowing that I'll never again ride across country, flying over jumps." Rafe stopped himself before he started complaining about not being able to walk up stairs, or easily navigate rough countryside. He used to be an outdoorsy person and now he felt confined to flat surfaces with chairs nearby for when his leg became tired. "But you've shown me it's not all bad. I'm lucky to have a good family, wonderful friends, and excellent food." Rafe had another mouthful of the gratin and washed it down with a sip of the crisp white wine James had poured earlier.

"Eat up and enjoy. Stewart will be in shortly with the ham."

"Oh yes, the ham. I do hope it lives up to the effort you went to in acquiring it."

James' cheeks blazed with colour and Rafe almost forgot that he'd decided not to kiss him. Had he made a mistake?

CHAPTER NINE

J ames leaned against the kitchen door as Cook sliced up the remaining ham and made little parcels to be given to all the staff at Beaumount Stud. He'd deliberately ordered much more than Rafe and himself could eat last night at the 1916 re-enactment dinner.

"This one is for Frank and the new lad." Cook handed him a basket filled with tinfoil wrapped parcels.

"Thank you. The new lad is named Johnny; he's the son of Nell's war captain." His sister's letter had been vague. She'd telegrammed Father asking for some documents, and then had sent this young lad to the farm. James was grateful. It was hard to find staff with so many lost in the war and to the flu, and the lad was keen to learn and was a natural with the horses. "Now for tomorrow, I want to do a special welcome home to England 1917 Christmas dinner, but with the leftover ham because of rations. Rafe was home by then…" James let his voice fade off, remembering the telegram and how he'd been too timid to visit. Afraid that his friend had changed and that they wouldn't have the same easy friendship as before the war. Now he knew he'd been correct, Rafe had changed. He was more attractive than before with his gruff temper, clear way of viewing reality, and the silvered touches at his temples. The war had taken his easy charm and hardened it, rather like a blacksmith's forge hardens and shapes metal.

"Is he enjoying these dinners? Much of the ham last night was uneaten."

"Honestly, it's hard to know. He's not as talkative as before the war." James paused for a second. "I mean, it's understandable. He's been through a lot and…"

Cook nodded. "Yes, you grew up with your issues. His were acquired suddenly."

"And not by his choice. I know. I understand his frustration with the families too. They've all told him to visit me because I'll understand, but I can't possibly understand. I'm more likely to see the differences between us than the similarities."

"Is that why you didn't visit me?" Rafe asked and James spun around. The basket of food whacked into the wall with a thud and threw him off balance. He dropped the basket, using his now free hand to grab the wall and keep himself upright.

"How much did you hear?" And why hadn't James noticed Rafe arriving in the hallway? He usually felt the air change whenever Rafe was near.

"What sort of question is that? It implies you don't want me to know what you said before you knew I might be listening."

James shook his head, hard enough to rattle his brain.

RENÉE DAHLIA

"No. It's not that. I... I've been trying to articulate why I didn't visit you when you were first injured."

"Because I was at the Clearing Station in Varennes. How could you have travelled there?"

Cook picked up the basket. "Now, now, young Rafael. There's no need to be mean."

"Now you are in trouble." James jabbed Rafe with his elbow and they both laughed. A smear of sensation flowed up James' arm into his shoulder and he breathed out, almost in relief, that Rafe's touch still affected him that way.

"God, Cook, you make me feel like I'm twelve again."

"And so I should. James here has gone to a lot of effort to make you feel at home, and you sneer at him with your nonsense about him not going to wherever you said."

"The Clearing Station at Varennes. It's a small town in France near the western front. I was... hurt near there. Spent fuck knows, my apologies, Cook. I mean, I don't know how long I was there, until the doctors sent me onwards to another hospital. I begged them to send me to Remys Station, where Mother and Luciana were, but that's not how the system works."

Cook frowned and James automatically rubbed his own forehead.

"Don't look at me like that. Family doesn't come first in the army. Obviously I wasn't going to heal enough to return to battle, so I wasn't a priority. And from what Mother told me later, when she arrived home from Remys, neither her nor Luciana would have time to care for me." Rafe scoffed. "Apparently the army did know best."

"Just because it's logical doesn't make it hurt any less,"

Cook said, and Rafe nodded at her soothing tone. If only it worked that way, and James' chest didn't ache over the image of Rafe lying alone, injured, in a temporary hospital bed on foreign lands.

"I remember reading your name in the paper under the casualties list. But they didn't say anything about where you were hurt, or where you'd be sent. I wanted to visit, to do more than send you a letter..." James let his voice fade off. If he'd really tried, his own father could have found out the information. Lord St. George still had contacts in the war office from his own youth, but James had been too afraid to ask. It was easier to keep sending his monthly letter to Rafe's regiment and let the army forward it to him.

"And yet, you didn't visit once you knew I was back in England."

"No. I didn't."

"Was it a bad journey home?" Cook asked and James wanted to both thank her for changing the subject and curse her for the same. He wished he had a ready explanation for his cowardly actions, one that painted him in a better light than the dull truth. He was scared he'd reveal his feelings if he'd visited. Rafe leaned against the wall opposite James. The end of one of his crutches touched the end of James' cane, and a tiny vibration travelled up the cane into James' hand.

"Bad is relative, I suppose," Rafe mused. "From Varennes, they put me on a train with a batch of other injured solders and some nurses who were transferring off the front line for a while. One of the nurses said we were going to Le Havre on the coast, about five hours train ride away."

"Five hours isn't too bad." James had imagined something much more strenuous.

Rafe laughed bitterly. "You imagine lying on the lowest bunk bed staring up at the bunk above you, hoping it'd been built properly and wouldn't fall on you."

"Oh?"

"The nurses said we were lucky. Some patients were sent to the coast in makeshift cattle cars on wooden benches. We managed to score a proper medical train with thirty-six patients per coach, with proper beds set up into three layered bunk beds."

"Would you rather have had the top?"

Rafe shook his head. "Couldn't get up that high. And the middle one folded up when it wasn't in use, so it was uncomfortable. I guess I ended up in the best place, except I had to worry they'd all land on me every time the train wobbled a bit."

"But only for five hours." James didn't think that was too bad in the scheme of things, but when Rafe laughed too loud, he gaped at him. "What?"

"Five hours. They told us it would be five hours. More like a day and a half."

"What? Why so long?" James fiddled with the hem on the pocket of his trousers.

Rafe shrugged. "The war. Injured soldiers aren't priority and we had to keep pulling into sidings to let more important trains through."

"Oh. I'm sorry. I should've realised."

Rafe sneered. "How could you have realised? You, who had all of this..."

"Have a care, Rafael." Cook remonstrated Rafe and he puffed out a short breath.

"I'm glad you could be naïve about the war, James. I really am, but damn if it makes me bloody jealous too. Sorry, Cook."

"Don't be sorry. We are very proud of your service, Rafe."

"Oh, now he's Rafe?" James scoffed and Rafe chuckled properly, not the mean hard laughter of before. "It's true though. We are all proud of you Rafe. Britain won the war because of good men like you."

"I wouldn't overstate it that much. I'm not a good man, just one who did his job until he couldn't."

"Don't you make me correct you again, Rafael," Cook brandished her wooden spoon in his direction.

James picked up the basket. "That was short lived. Come along, Rafe, let's deliver these hams to Frank and the new lad."

James pulled on a clean shirt and brushed his hair for dinner. Yesterday, he'd spent the day with Rafe at his side over at the stables. Frank had brought in all the broodmares with foals at foot, and James had spent the day inspecting them and assisting with the first stage of weaning for the older foals, those that were six months old. The late foals would stay with their dams for another month or two, until their mothers became tired of them and started to self-wean them. Since the older foals had already reached that phase, the first step of weaning went smoothly with the new herds of young horses split out into colts and fillies and sent into fresh paddocks with an old retired gelding or aged broodmare for each mob to look after them. With most of his retired horses sent to war, the mobs were bigger than he'd prefer, but needs must.

His hands shook a little as he buttoned up his shirt—tonight was the 1917 dinner—Rafe had been back in England. James had gone to Scotland for Christmas with his cousins, and yes, he'd used that as an excuse to avoid his friend. He'd still written his letters diligently though. Did that count?

There was a knock at the door.

"Yes?"

"It's me." Rafe called out and James invited him in.

"Is there a problem?"

Rafe stood awkwardly, stiffer than usual. "I've been thinking about dinner tonight."

"And?"

"Perhaps we should sit down?" Rafe didn't sit in the chair in the corner of the room, but instead sat on the end of James' bed. James' heart stopped, then accelerated, like a horse standing behind the barrier rope, then surging forward when the rope went up. So many times he'd imagined Rafe on his bed and now it was really happening. Rafe; in his room. On his bed. Staring at him with what James hoped was lust.

"What is the problem?" James realised he had his fist pressed against his breastbone and he dropped it to his side. Rafe cleared his throat. Was he nervous too? James glanced at the bed, then at the chair, unsure about what to do.

"The dinner tonight. It's for 1917, yes?"

"Yes."

Rafe nodded, too many times. "Um, yes. Well, I guess you could say that 1917 was a homecoming year for me. In 1916, I spent Christmas at the No2 General Hospital in Le Havre. I had to have several operations to remove shrapnel from my leg and torso and it took many months before the doctors thought I would cope with the boat ride home. Eventually, I was put on a boat and sent to Southhampton, then on a train to London, before another train to Chesterfield. Father collected me in a very fancy new car and drove me home to Stanmore."

"It was Easter. I remember your father called mine on the telephone." Beaumount Stud had installed a telephone in 1905, one of the earliest ones in Newmarket. The racecourse had had a special business line installed when James was a child and since then several of the bigger stud farms had installed private lines.

"That sounds like something he would have done. Please can you sit down and stop hovering?"

James blinked. "I've been hovering?"

Rafe patted the bed beside him and a rush of heat flushed over James' skin. "Yes. Look, I've let myself get distracted—"

"Have you?" James was certainly not thinking about talking anymore.

"Yes. I wanted to talk about 1917 and the idea of home-coming." Rafe paused. "Damn it, can you please sit down?"

"Fine." James grabbed the wooden chair beside his dresser with one hand and swung it around so he could sit down.

"1917 was a year of home coming for me, and I've been thinking about that."

"So you just said."

"James." Rafe growled.

"What?"

Rafe threaded his hands through his hair and glared at James. The fierce look only increased the heat in his veins. "You said you've been wooing me and damn it, I've been trying to tell you that it's working."

James couldn't move. It was as if Rafe's comment had glued his legs to the chair. He felt like if he leaned forward to stand up, he'd topple over.

"James? Can you stop staring at me like that and say something?"

"Ummm." James opened and shut his mouth several times.

"Anything?"

"I don't understand."

Rafe pushed his hands through his hair again. "It was the homecoming. I realised that I hadn't come home properly. Not until I was here. It's a bad bargain for you. I'm not the charming larrikin I was before the war. There isn't even all of me here—"

"As I care about that, Rafe."

"The grumps or the missing leg?"

"Both. Neither."

Rafe glared. "Don't you dare say it's irrelevant."

"Of course it's not fucking irrelevant. What I meant was that my feelings don't care about your war scars—inside or out. I still want you." James stood up, hands on hips and gave Rafe his most fierce glare to match the one of Rafe's face.

"Good. Because I'm home now. Being with you is home." Rafe's declaration stole all of James' breath, stunning him more than a smack in the chops with a sodden mop would do. Everything he'd ever wanted was here in this room, and he could barely believe it. For years, he'd lusted after Rafe and had resigned himself to being only his friend. Could he forgive himself for not being brave enough to take this final step and accept Rafe's declaration?

CHAPTER TEN

Rafe held his breath as he declared himself to James. He'd spent all day imagining how this would go, and he'd been so impossibly wrong. James had told him he wanted kisses, and more, so naturally Rafe assumed he'd fall at Rafe's feet. But no. James just stared at him with those hazel eyes flared wide.

"I always forget how tall you are." Rafe had to break the tension in the room and all he could manage was repeating the awkward thing he'd said before.

"What?" James shook his head once as if trying to clear cobwebs. Then he rubbed his eyes. "Did you just say that you want to stay here? With me?"

"No." It wasn't the place Rafe wanted, it was James. Home was anywhere with James, but he didn't get to explain because James yelled.

"What?" James flung his arms wide. "What?" he whispered, and collapsed back into the chair, his head in his hands.

"I didn't say I wanted to stay here with you, although of

course that is what I want. I said I'm home now. I want to build a home with you... If you'll have me."

James dropped his hands away from his face. "If I'll have you? I've spent years writing you letters hinting at my feelings for you."

"I missed all your hints." Rafe had spent most of the day reading James' old letters and the depth of James' love for him was apparent. At least, as soon as he knew what he was looking at. The entirety of his outpouring of affection made Rafe feel rather clumsy for not noticing.

"Well, damn it, the law doesn't exactly make it easy." James wiped his hands on his pants. "Why do you think I've spent the last few weeks wooing you with faked Christmas dinners. I've been trying to convince you to be with me. All that effort, and you still doubt whether I'd have you?"

"When you put it that way..." Rafe breathed out, a long passage of air that emptied his lungs. "Please kiss me."

James leaped to his feet and somehow managed to fall forward onto the bed beside Rafe. It was easy to roll with the motion of James' body, and when they stopped moving, Rafe lay on top of James. Heaven. Having James underneath him was everything he didn't know he'd wanted. No, that was a lie. He'd wanted this for a fucking long time. Other soldiers had talked about near death experiences which involved bright lights and floating sensations. He'd scoffed at them, calling it nonsense, but now he understood. It wasn't a near death experience. It was the highest peak of life. Every vein, every nerve, every piece of skin on his body hummed and glowed as if he were filled with light and it shone out of him.

"You alright?" James sounded a bit muffled and Rafe raised his head.

"Yes." More than alright, just unable to express the moment and how it was burning itself onto his flesh, like a branding iron. He half-expected his skin to be permanently marked with James' form.

"Will you kiss me, then?"

Rafe shifted and placed more of his weight on his arms. All the details began to emerge, as if from a fog, a haze of sensation, how his shoulders were broader than James' but not by much, how his foot didn't quite reach James' ankles. How James' hair and face and lips were right there, right beside his own face and it would take only the tiniest movement to kiss him.

"I think I will. Would you like me to kiss you?"

James' mouth parted slightly, his tongue darting across his lower lip. "Yes please."

Rafe bent his head to close the gap between them and touched his lips to James. Home. This was where he had always wanted to be. James tasted like mint and pepper, with a hint of cloves, like an evening cocktail. Luxurious and yet homely, because Rafe had found his place in the world. James threaded his fingers into Rafe's hair and pulled him closer, deepening the kiss. He cupped James' stubble roughened cheek, the texture of his skin on Rafe's palm adding to the flourish of desire now spreading through his body. When James stroked his tongue with his own, Rafe couldn't go slow anymore. There would be no more waiting, no more holding back from his future. This wasn't a moment in time, but the beginning of the rest of his life. He clung to James with one hand, the other exploring his body, down his arms over biceps, forearms, hands with just the perfect smattering of hair over the back of them, and back to his throat. Rafe stroked down the column of James' throat to that pesky button on his shirt hiding Rafe's favourite little spot. And all the while, kissing and kissing because he needed more of James' mouth. More of his taste. James pushed gently and together they rolled onto their sides, freeing up hands to explore. Rafe knew exactly what he wanted, and his fingers fumbled on the top button of James' shirt. It took far too long to flick the pesky button out of its hole and expose James' throat. Oh, but when he managed it, he smiled.

"What's so funny?"

"Nothing is funny."

"Why the smile?"

Rafe winked. "You'll see." He dragged his lips down James' throat, down to that little spot at the base of his throat where he could see the skin moving up and down as James breathed, slightly ragged to match Rafe's own desperate pants. He pressed his lips there and licked. A hint of salt mingled with the rest of the flavours on Rafe's tongue. He hummed in satisfaction, knowing his lips would vibrate on James' skin.

"Do that again."

Rafe complied, then mumbled against James. "That's why I smiled. Smug satisfaction."

"I'll give you satisfaction."

Rafe jerked his head up to stare at James. "I fucking hope so." James' gaze darkened and Rafe pushed him back onto his back. He ripped off his shirt, buttons flying, and spread it wide to expose James' chest. James was strong and lean with a dusting of light brown hairs over his chest. Rafe could spend hours dedicated to that chest, but not yet. Not when there were better prizes. He flicked one of James' nipples and James chuckled.

"That does nothing for me."

"Oh, that's a shame. I rather like it." Rafe loved it when someone pinched his nipples hard. One day; and he could see the calculation on James' face as he stored away the little snippet.

"But first..." Rafe stroked his hands over James' body, down his stomach. Each muscle tightened a bit as he slid his hands over them, until he traced his fingers over the trail of hair leading from James' belly button down lower to the promise of pleasure. Ha.

"What is funny now?" James' strangled tone tore Rafe's attention away from his task.

Rafe coughed awkwardly. "I suppose I have to share now, even though it's not the greatest timing."

James ruffled Rafe's hair. "Don't say I reminded you of a former lover... because that's weird."

"No. A soldier I knew, but not in that way unfortunately. He had a rather spectacular body, and knew it, but had no interest in men."

"Oh?"

Rafe spent a silent few moments undoing James' pants, his fingers slick with the sweat of anticipation.

"Come on. Tell me." James tugged at Rafe's hair and little prickles spread over his skull. His pulse quickened faster than Rafe thought possible.

"Fine. Corporal Walker used to call his cock the promise of pleasure and..."

James laughed. "Fucking what?"

"I know. I know. It's..."

"A bit of a strange time to remember something like that."

Rafe's throat thickened and he coughed again. Had he only thought the phrase, not said it, and now the story was without context? "To be clear, I never had sex with Corporal Walker. He wasn't interested in men, or me, although he certainly filled my fantasies. He used to strut around the camp with no shirt and his thumbs caught in his pants..."

"That's quite the image."

"Yeah, until you listened to his nonsense. He talked constantly about visiting whores and giving them a taste of his promise of pleasure."

"His promise of pleasure?" James laughed.

Rafe breathed out. "He was quite full of himself and probably got VD in his first week in France. Anyway, it's not so much that you remind me of him—"

"Thank God."

Rafe chuckled. "More that my hands spread over your stomach reminded me of the way he held his hands, and then his saying popped into my brain... For the first time ever, I understood what he meant."

"You'll promise me pleasure, or I am the promise of pleasure?"

"Both, dear James. Both." Rafe kissed James hard on the mouth, a full wrestle of a kiss that begged and commanded. He poured all his long pent up desire into the kiss because the only reason he'd wanted to wait was because James deserved more than a quick fuck from a grumpy soldier. There wasn't a good reason for him to change his mind, except for James. James was the reason—he'd gone on a campaign to woo Rafe—beginning before the war had begun, and Rafe was only know realising how extensive and persuasive James had been. It was the bloody ham that tipped him over. Even after he'd told James to wait, James had quietly continued to woo him every day. Unstopped by Rafe's gruffness, James kept reaching out and showing Rafe his love with small gestures. And now James kissed back with the same desperation. Rafe's hands slid over James' body, across his chest, down his sides, everywhere, until he grabbed James' pants and tugged them down. James spoke something into their kiss, but their joined lips muffled it. Rafe followed the path of his hand with his mouth, licking his way over James' torso.

"You'll have to help me."

"With?"

"My left hip doesn't have the same flex as the right."

Rafe glanced up. "I'll take care of you."

"Keep talking like that and I'll spill in my pants before you touch me."

"I am touching you." Rafe gripped James' waist tighter to prove his point.

"Yeah, but not on my cock."

"Would you like me to..."

James' breath whistled. "Yes please. Touch my cock, Rafe."

"With pleasure."

James huffed out a breath that was almost a laugh. "Promise?"

Rafe buried his face against James' stomach and let out the laughter until his shoulders shook. The release of tension was fucking perfect and his whole body became lighter and hotter. Ready. It was easy work to help James lift his hips and pull his pants down his legs. The brief flash of sadness at his own lost leg came and went faster than the fucking shell that had blown him up. Rafe resigned himself to always having that response and he shook his head to clear it away. Other people said it would fade with time. He wasn't so sure about that—so much of his pre-war identity had been wrapped up in his physicality, he knew it would take a long time to find a new identity. A new reason to be proud of himself. He hadn't wanted to involve James in that journey, mostly because he wasn't sure James would stick by him, but James kept proving he would and today Rafe made a conscious decision to trust James and his intentions. Rafe never doubted James, only himself, and the moment he'd realised the difference, he knew this was where he needed to be.

James grabbed Rafe's hands and guided them to his cock, thick and hard, and Rafe realised he'd frozen still while contemplating life. Existential problems could be dealt with later, because when Rafe wrapped his fingers around the smooth skin of James' cock, all his problems faded away. All his attention focused on the beautiful rod before him.

"God James. If I'd known you were hiding this in your pants, I would've done this years ago."

James chuckled, a gentle encouraging laugh, that halted on a strangled yelp as Rafe slid his hand up and down James' shaft. He took his time, lavishing James with attention until James begged him to stop.

"Do you have some of that massage oil?"

"In my bedside drawer." James croaked and vaguely waved one hand in that direction. His loose relaxed movement made Rafe smile as he moved across the bed towards the drawer. The little jar sat there within easy reach.

"Now roll over onto your stomach."

"Like this?" James rolled over and curved his spine so his arse rose up temptingly into the air.

Rafe patted the round muscle. "Tease."

"Only for you." James turned his head and smiled.

"I should kiss you for that."

"Or you could..." James wriggled his butt and the way he moved, slightly off-centre, was so fucking perfectly James that Rafe's cock rubbed eagerly against his pants. He placed the little jar beside James and rolled onto his back so he could pull his own pants off. From this angle, James wouldn't see his scars. Rafe dragged in a deep breath—James had already seen them and hadn't flinched—that's why this was fine. James accepted him before he had, and what a gift that was.

"What are you doing back there?"

"Be patient." Rafe patted James' arse again.

"Harder."

Rafe obliged, slapping the taut muscle but not hard enough to leave a mark. Only a slight pink smudge. "Like that?" The groan from James was enough of an answer. But Rafe wouldn't do it again. He wasn't into handing out pain to someone, although he did like it when others pushed that boundary of pleasure and pain for him. Just the idea of having

James bite his nipples made him shiver. He undid the lid on the jar and scooped a handful of the jellied oil onto his hand. Tossing aside the jar, he rubbed his hands together to warm the oil. It melted at his touch, releasing a rosehip perfume into the air, and before James could beg him again, he spread the oil over James' buttocks. Every stroke of the muscles created a groan from James, and Rafe could do this for hours.

"Please Rafe."

"You want me?"

James's voice was rough, throaty. "Yes. Rafe. Please fuck me." He spread his legs wider, opening his hole for Rafe. Rafe spread the oil over the puckered hole and pressed one finger inside. If he could own the sound James made, he'd pay everything for it.

"Like this?"

"Yes. More."

Rafe took his time, getting James ready, until he was slick, panting, and begging for him. Then he shifted his body, his knee pressing deep into the bed. The position wasn't as easy as it had been in the past, and he needed to balance across James with his weight on his leg and the opposite arm. It meant guiding his cock into James was a bit of a mission and his body shook with the effort. One hand on his cock, the other holding him in place, and only one leg to balance.

"Now. More. Rafe." James cried out his name on a long syllable and Rafe almost cursed as he tried to navigate himself. For a moment he felt like a virginal youth, unsure of himself, but as soon as he pressed the tip of his cock into James, all of that fled. He used his weight to press James into the bed and with the change of angle, he didn't need his missing leg for balance anymore. This worked for him, and judging by the soft moans from James, it worked for him too. Slowly, he buried himself deep inside James and truly knew he was home.

"Rafe. I need you." James' hands spread on the bed, his fingers wide apart, as Rafe began to thrust. Gently at first, then as James begged, harder and harder. He slid one hand under James' body, curling his fingers around James' cock, then buried his face against James' shoulder. Together they came on a shout that mixed and mingled in the air, both voices combined. Rafe's body shook with the final tremors and he collapsed onto James. Home.

CHAPTER ELEVEN

James waited as Stewart carved the leftover ham and tried to hold back the joyful smile that kept threatening to break out across his face. Surely he could manage to have proper manners for a few more minutes, at least until Stewart left the room, and he'd be able to grin happily at his lover and best friend. Rafe. Eventually Stewart completed his task, handed out their dinners with food piled high. James' stomach grumbled as the rich scents of the food rose up off his plate.

"Hungry?" Rafe asked.

"Yes, I must have done some strenuous exercise today."

The way Rafe blushed warmed James all the way through, and it wasn't until the door banged slightly that he realised he'd held Rafe's gaze not noticing Stewart's departure.

"Careful. You'll have everyone talking about us." Rafe grinned.

James shrugged one shoulder. "The staff have already

heard the rumours about me. If they have a problem with my... inclinations, they would have left a long time ago."

"You trust them?"

"I have to. I'm not the only person in Newmarket guarding a secret like this. I read the papers too, and the damned Billing "Forty-Seven Thousand" case didn't help at all, but his anti-Semitism also has people wary of his ideas. He paints himself as a hero, of course, but don't all villains with terrible ideas?" James didn't want to talk politics, especially not when Billing had the popular vote and too many people agreed with his nonsense. He was fortunate to have a family who disagreed with Billing and allowed love of all types to thrive; and even luckier to live in Newmarket where the only currency that mattered was good horsemanship. What people did in the privacy of their own homes was no one's business, provided they looked after their horses properly. Owners were valued by their ability to pay their bills on time. Racing had always been a bit of a safe haven for those who didn't belong in polite society; for the grifters who wanted to get ahead, and for those gambled on life and love.

Silence descended, and James cut into his ham. After a few minutes, the awkwardness between them began to make him feel twitchy.

"I ordered the ham again because in 1917, rationing had begun and I wanted to get the sense of how difficult that was for everyone." Rationing was a duller topic than the legalities of his feelings, but one that could be discussed openly. James had spent most of his life writing to Rafe with guarded expressions of love and lust, and those habits would keep them both safe from prison.

"Difficult?"

"Yes. At the start of 1917, rationing was voluntary, and it didn't really affect us here on the farm, although wheat and therefore bread became expensive. But by Christmas, the Germans had been quite successful with their submarines and had sunk many ships bringing in wheat, so rationing became compulsory. Even here on the farm, where we grow a lot of our food, we had to comply with the system."

"Couldn't you sell some produce to compensate?"

"Yes. We were already doing that, and we'd planted out many of the paddocks into food crops, rather than leave them for the horses. We'd ended up selling off most of our young stock and all our retired geldings to the army, so we had less stock on the farm anyway."

"Meanwhile, I was lying in a hospital bed in Le Havre, unsure if I'd ever see English soil again."

James drew a deep breath into his lungs. "I'm so fucking glad you did."

"So am I. I know I held you at arms length even after your confession, and I'm sorry for that."

James stood up, needing to hold Rafe and reassure him.

"No, please sit."

He sat.

"I was scared, James. Scared of hurting you. Scared of being hurt. But when I saw you with Cook making little parcels of leftovers for your staff, I knew that you would never hurt me."

"Not intentionally, no."

Rafe squared his shoulders and blew out a short breath. "That left only one thing holding me back. Myself. I've changed since the war. Not just on the outside... Really the external changes are the less dramatic ones."

"But at your core, you are still you."

"A grumpier, jumpier me. They call it shell shock. I don't cope well with loud noises, even the banging of a door closing makes my muscles jerk. I have these nightmares where I lash out. Honestly, I don't trust myself to sleep in the same bed as you."

A rush of heat filled James' body. "Now there's a way to shock the staff."

But Rafe only shook his head, his eyes filled with sadness. "I'd love to sleep with you. I want to be with you, but I might hurt you. I've woken up with torn blankets, and things thrown across the room and no memory of it. I don't trust my sleeping self."

"Then we won't sleep in the same bed. I'll do whatever you need." James sounded desperate and needy and he bowed his head.

"I think I just need time. Is that going to be enough for you?"

"Rafe. No. It's not going to be enough for me."

"Excuse me?"

"Because you are already everything to me. If you need time, then take it. I want to spend the rest of my life with you. If you want that too, then we have time to figure out how to be together. So no, you aren't simply enough for me, you are more than that."

Rafe rubbed his cheekbone. "I don't deserve you."

"Oh yes you do. Don't you dare say that." James stood up. "Rafe. I didn't visit you when you came home to England because I thought I didn't deserve you. You went to war, you sacrificed for our country. What did I do? Sit here in my expensive house surrounded by luxuries. I didn't deserve you and I punished myself for it. And for what? I could have kissed you over a year ago. We've already missed all that time together because I thought I didn't deserve you."

"You were wrong."

"I know that now. And that's why I know that you deserve me too." James sat in Rafe's lap and kissed him, uncaring if Cook or Stewart saw them. Rafe was his forever.

"Will it scandalise everyone if I move in?"

James chuckled. "Right now, sitting here in your arms, I can't find it in myself to care. I've always loved you Rafe, for as long as I can remember. You are my best friend and the most incredible man I've ever met."

Rafe's arms tightened around him. "I've fought so hard against wanting you. And you kept reminding me that I didn't need to. I'm glad you persisted because I love you, you stubborn darling man."

Thank you for reading HIS LORD'S SOLDIER, the final book in my Great War series.

Want a bit more romance and to find out how all the characters in the Great War series are getting on in 1921? An extended epilogue is available as an exclusive bonus when you sign up for my newsletter.

If you love reading mm romance, my new Gamble Racing series is set in the world of Formula One car racing. DRIVEN TO DISTRACTION will release in November 2022.

A race to the finish line, and a family secret ...

F1 driver Ondrej D'Grieg has one goal in life. Be a champion. To achieve that he needs to focus. That's why Ondrej has no time for his father's insistence on him being involved with some old family drama about a missing rare car. He can ignore the mystery, but Hudson, the historian investigating, is more than a little distracting.

Hudson Lockley has a research job to do, and falling for the son of his employer is a no-no. But only one thing is more fascinating than this puzzle; Mr D'Grieg's famous racing car driver son, Ondrej.

When their interest turns to kisses, then more, the race to figure out this attraction between them starts. But a small mistake could cause a crash that breaks both their hearts.

If you are new to the Great War series, the first book is HER LADY'S MELODY.

An aristocrat hiding from her past, a doctor hiding from her grief, a journey that will be a danger to themselves... and their hearts!

War doctor Luciana Stanmore was not healed by the singing of the armistice last year. Unable to face returning to England without the lover the war took from her, she goes instead to seek comfort with her grandmother in Amsterdam, where the beautiful widow next door catches her eye.

If anyone discovers Therese de Seletsky's identity, it would be all over for her Russian aristocrat son. She lost her husband to the Bolsheviks and she'll do anything to keep Pavel safe, including denying her own need for music and love. When he breaks his arm playing, Therese risks accepting the help of her mysterious new neighbour, and ignores the tug of attraction between them.

An attempted kidnap of Pavel changes everything. Therese can only turn to Luciana, and England, to unlock the secret of why she's being targeted. Along the way, they draw closer, but how can they love when the pain of the past is a present threat?

A steamy girl next door lesbian story of yearning, hope, and new love after loss. HEA guaranteed.

ACKNOWLEDGMENTS

I pay my respects to the Wangal people of the Eora Nation, who are the traditional owners of the land on which this book was written.

Thank you to all the wonderful readers who have read this series so far. I appreciate every review and the time readers have given to creating reviews.

AUTHOR NOTES

The first act of parliament to outlaw homosexuality in England was the Buggery Act of 1553 and convictions were punishable by death. This was downgraded in 1861 to ten years imprisonment with the Offences Against The Person Act, but in 1885, the Criminal Law Amendment Act made any homosexual act illegal, even those in private homes. Known as the Blackmailer's Charter, it was ambiguously worded and any letter could be used as 'evidence.' In 1895, Oscar Wilde was prosecuted under this act. By contrast, lesbian acts of homosexuality were never explicitly covered in any legislation (presumably because these laws were written by men and assumed a male perspective?). A Bill was introduced in 1921 to include women but was rejected on the basis that it might encourage women to explore homosexuality. More author notes can be found on my website.

ALL BOOKS BY RENÉE DAHLIA

Thanks for reading HIS LORD'S SOLDIER. I hope you enjoyed it.

Reviews can help readers find books, and I am grateful for all honest reviews. Thank you for taking the time to let others know what you've read, and what you thought.

If you write a review for HIS LORD'S SOLDIER and email me I will send you a free copy of any of my other books of your choice. My email is renee@reneedahlia.com.

If you'd like to know more about me, my books, or to connect with me online, you can visit my webpage www.reneedahlia.com and if you sign up to my newsletter, you can grab a free book.

Twitter https://twitter.com/dekabat
Facebook https://www.facebook.com/
reneedahliawriter/
Instagram https://www.instagram.com/
reneedahlia_author/
Patreon https://www.patreon.com/reneedahlia
BookBub https://www.bookbub.com/authors/
renee-dahlia

Historical Series: Great War

1. Her Lady's Melody (ff)
2. Her Lady's Fortune (ff)
3. Her Lady's Honor (ff)
4. His Lord's Soldier (mm)

Historical Series: Desiring the Dexingtons

1. Love Wasn't Built in a Day (mm)
2. The Secret Life of Spinsters (ff)
3. The Widow's Modiste (ff)

Historical Series: Great War

1. Her Lady's Melody (ff)
2. Her Lady's Fortune (ff)
3. Her Lady's Honor (ff)
4. His Lord's Soldier (mm)

Historical Series: Bluestockings

Prequel: The Shipwrecked Earl's Bride (fm with bisexual hero)

1. To Charm a Bluestocking (fm with bisexual hero)
2. In Pursuit of a Bluestocking (fm)
3. The Heart of a Bluestocking (fm)

Contemporary Series: Gamble Racing

1. Driven to Distraction (mm)
2. Driven by Passion (mm)
3. Driven by Ambition (mm)
4. Driven to Protect (mm)

Contemporary Series: Seraph's Burlesque Club

1. Show Up (ff with bisexual heroine)
2. Show Off (ff with bisexual heroines)
3. Show Queen (ff)
4. Show Time (mm)
5. Show Dance (mm)

Contemporary Series: Kapow!

1. Out of Her League (fm with bisexual characters)
2. His Buxom Beauty (fm)
3. Craving His Spotlight (mm)
4. Her Pregnant Rival (ff)

Contemporary Series: Farrellton Foster Family

1. Betrayed (fm)
2. Forbidden (fm with bisexual characters)
3. Liability (ff)

Contemporary Series: Margaret River TV: Boxed Set

- Homage (fm with bisexual heroine)
- Uplift (ff with bisexual heroines)

Contemporary Series: Merindah Park

1. Merindah Park (fm)
2. Making Her Mark (fm with bisexual heroine)
3. Two Hearts Healing (fm)
4. Racetrack Royalty (fm)

Contemporary Series: Rainbow Cove

1. His Christmas Pearl (fm)
2. His Christmas Pride (mm)